GREG FOSTER becomes livid with rage when he thinks of all the men Gwen has been with—yet he wants to believe he can change her, that she can be his alone.

GWEN SHERMAN longs for respectability, but will her love for Greg be enough to wipe out the shadows of her past?

PHILLIP CHANCELLOR is consumed with passion for a vivacious, younger woman. What will his wife do when she finds out?

JILL FOSTER falls eagerly into Phillip's arms—he has so much to offer a girl, especially one from the wrong side of the tracks.

———————

Series Story Editor **Mary Ann Cooper** is America's foremost soap opera expert. She writes the nationally syndicated column *Speaking of Soaps*, is a major contributor to leading soap opera magazines, and is a radio and television personality.

Angelica Aimes, who wrote *Echoes of Love* is the well-known romance w̶r̶i̶t̶ *Divided Heart* and New Englander between her M secluded island i

D1430493

Dear Friend,

Just when things are going along so well, something happens to take the wind out of your sails. Isn't that the way it always seems? Leslie Brooks had blossomed as a woman and had also become an accomplished musician. She enjoyed the love and respect of a wonderful man. In Book 3, *Echoes of Love*, Leslie can't foresee that her life is about to take a detour.

Meanwhile, Greg Foster finds himself at odds with his brother, Snapper, over Chris Brooks. The Foster family has gone through many hard times, yet they've managed to remain a close-knit unit. Will their love of the same woman drive two brothers apart?

In upcoming Soaps & Serials novelizations you'll see that feuds never last very long in the Foster and Brooks families.

For Soaps & Serials Books,

Mary Ann Cooper

Mary Ann Cooper

P.S. If you missed Books 1 and 2 of this series, see the order form on page 192 which also tells you how to order books in our other Soaps & Serials™ paperback series.

The Young and the Restless

ECHOES OF LOVE

William J. Bell and Lee Phillip Bell, Co-Creators,
Executive Producers, and Head Writers

&Soaps™ &Serials

PIONEER COMMUNICATIONS NETWORK, INC.

Echoes of Love

THE YOUNG AND THE RESTLESS paperback novels are published and distributed by Pioneer Communications Network, Inc.

SOAPS & SERIALS™ is a trademark of Pioneer Communications Network, Inc.

ISBN: 0-916217-73-6

Printed in the United States of America

10 9 8 7 6 5 4 3 2 1

ECHOES OF LOVE

Chapter One

A Flame-Haired Beauty

Outside the window of the Genoa City legal aid office the sky was a robin's egg blue with only the faintest white threads of clouds. The trees were thick with supple green leaves, and the intoxicating fragrance of newly mown grass wafted through the open window filling Greg Foster's mind with dreams of leisurely picnics in mossy groves, a fun loving girl with strawberry blonde hair and eyes as blue as the sky looking up at him, a special smile turning up the edges of her tempting lips. It couldn't be just any girl, but one perfect girl—Chris Brooks Foster, his sister-in-law.

Although the seasons had changed from winter to spring and now to early summer since he'd lost Chris to his brother, Snapper, Greg's heart had not thawed with the weather. His love was so strong that it had frozen his heart, making every other girl appear dull and ordinary by comparison. Even if he could never have Chris, he could still dream of her—and he did. Every night, and often during the day, his thoughts slid back to her.

Greg hadn't really lost Chris, because he'd never possessed her. All he had to cling to was a single kiss, but the sweet taste, the driving intensity of it had burned through his heart. If he had met her first, he thought despondently, Chris might have loved him instead of Snapper. But she had already been married to and separated from his brother when he got home from Yale Law School. It was just a lucky coincidence that she worked in the office beside his own—a coincidence that changed his life forever and spoiled every other girl for him. Instead of divorcing Snapper, as Greg had hoped she would, Chris refused to give up on her marriage. The vows she swore on her wedding day had been made with all her heart: "For better or for worse, until death do us part." Shaken by Greg's unexpected passion and by her response to it, Chris had gone back to Snapper determined to salvage what was left of their marriage before it was too late. And all Greg could do was wish them well.

"Err, errgh." Gwen Sherman cleared her throat loudly. "Well, Mr. Foster, have you decided whether you're going to take my case?"

Forcing his attention back to the client sitting across the desk from him, Greg answered brusquely, "Legal aid lawyers don't have a choice in the matter. I've been assigned to your case. So, like it or not, we're stuck with each other...and you might as well call me Greg. We're going to be spending a lot of time together, so let's get over the formalities right now."

"Sure, Greg," Gwen flashed an engaging smile at him and batted her long, black-mascaraed lashes. "Being stuck with you sounds just swell."

"Glad to hear that," Greg replied routinely. "Now why don't you tell me about your case. Start from the beginning..."

"But that's what I've been doing for the past forty-five minutes," Gwen protested.

"Sorry." Greg sounded as sheepish as he felt. "I guess my mind wandered. I'm a little preoccupied and..."

"Your girl tell you to take a hike?" Gwen interrupted.

"Not exactly, but close enough," Greg admitted. "How did you know?"

Gwen shrugged off his question. "Woman's intuition, I guess," she said. Actually, there wasn't much about men that she hadn't learned at too tender an age, but she wasn't going to admit that to the earnest young lawyer who was studying her now as if she'd just walked into his office.

It was true. Greg hadn't really looked at his client before. He'd been too preoccupied with thoughts of Chris to notice anyone else. Now, though, he focused intently on her. Gwen Sherman was balanced tensely on the edge of the chair, a practiced smile plastered firmly on her face as if she were a stewardess or beauty queen contestant. Her tight black leather skirt had ridden up, revealing an endless expanse of long, slender legs held tightly together and crossed demurely at the ankles; in her lap she clutched a black hobo shoulder bag as if she were afraid it might be snatched from her at any moment. Two plain gold chains hung down into the V neck of her fuzzy white angora sweater, too hot for even an early summer day like this one, Greg thought, but maybe she didn't have anything else to wear. It was obvious that she'd dressed with care to visit him; probably it was the first time she'd ever been in a lawyer's office. The thought softened his mood, and he smiled at her encouragingly. She was probably pretty enough, he decided critically, under the tons of make-up she'd applied with an over-liberal hand. But by far her most striking feature was the thick crown of red hair that framed her face and cascaded around her shoulders like a sunburst.

Patting it self-consciously as if she knew he'd been admiring it, Gwen said, "O.K., if I've got to start all over again, I may as well get on with it. What do you want to know?"

There was a trace of sullenness in her voice that didn't escape Greg's notice. "Listen, Gwen, I've got a better idea." He grinned boyishly, thoughts of idyllic summer picnics still lingering in the corners of his mind. "Since I've wasted so much of your time already, why don't we go out, grab a couple of sandwiches, find a bench in the park that the birds haven't already claimed, and then you can talk my ear off? I promise I'll listen to every word—scout's honor."

Scout's honor! Gwen couldn't believe her ears. The men she was used to dealing with never spoke like that. But Greg Foster probably had been a boy scout. And he probably still held the door open for a lady and helped old women cross the street. It never occurred to Gwen that in many ways Greg's life had been as tough as her own.

Pressured by the burden of debts and the needs of three growing children, his father had deserted the family—leaving his mother without a cent. Most of the burden had fallen on Greg's older brother, Snapper, who had felt obliged to take up the responsibilities his father had walked away from. But all the Fosters went to work after school and on weekends to help out, while at the same time also managing to keep up with their studies. Maybe they were determined not to end up like their father. Whatever their motivation, both the Foster boys had driven themselves to succeed—Snapper going to medical school and Greg winning a full scholarship to the prestigious Yale Law School. To Gwen Sherman, though, looking from the handsome young Ivy League lawyer to the impressive diploma framed on his wall, it seemed as if Greg Foster must be a charter member of that elite world of power and priviledge that she only knew from television and movies.

"Well, what do you say, Gwen?" Greg was smiling at her. "Have I got myself a deal?"

"I *am* a little hungry," she admitted grudgingly, worrying that the few dollars she had in her bag wouldn't be enough to pay for her share of lunch and the bus fare home. If she had to walk, she'd never make it in the spike heels she was wearing.

"Great, then let's go."

Grabbing his jacket and slinging it over his shoulder, Greg opened the door for Gwen. She teetered out ahead of him, displaying each of her assets clearly. Her heels made her almost as tall as he was, and her clinging sweater and skin tight skirt accentuated her statuesque figure. Other men would have responded with wolfish whistles, but Greg automatically compared her to Chris and was disappointed.

Seated on the park bench, though, a little while later, he found himself drawn into the story she was telling. Although she had insisted that all she wanted was a banana yogurt, Greg had ordered two thick roast beef sandwiches, pickles, potato salad, and four deviled eggs—just like a real picnic. Now the yogurt was forgotten and Gwen was devouring half of a sandwich—"just half," she'd insisted—as she talked.

"My folks have a farm in Indiana—not much of anything really," she said between bites. "But have you got any idea how hard you've got to work just to keep up a field of corn, a couple of scrawny cows, a few chickens, and a pig? Up at five every morning and not a day's vacation all year round. No sir, that was no life for me. I split out of there the first chance I got. I was fifteen then, and I've never been back."

"What made you choose Genoa City instead of Chicago or Detroit or some other big city?" Greg asked, laying the other half of the sandwich down on the bench beside her.

"It's such a pretty name, don't you think, Genoa City? Kind of exotic," Gwen chewed thoughtfully. "Besides, I had just enough money saved up for the ticket here."

"Was it a happy choice?"

"What do you mean?"

"I mean, coming to Genoa City?"

"Oh, sure, everything's been going along just swell, until I ran into this trouble with my landlord. I told you, he wants to evict me...put me out on the street, just because I'm late with the rent once in a while."

"Tell me again," Greg said, this time listening closely to every word she said. If he failed her, he knew she wouldn't have any other avenue of recourse. That was why he took his job so seriously and worked harder than a private lawyer who charged two hundred dollars an hour for each of his clients. Legal aid was the only hope for those people who couldn't afford an attorney's fees.

Gwen bit into the second half of the sandwich, hoping that Greg wouldn't think she always ate so much. Her landlord wanted her out because he suspected what her true occupation was, but she didn't want to admit that to her clean-cut, all-American lawyer. After all, Gwen told herself, she was only doing it until she got on her feet. The first time she'd told herself that had been five years ago, when she ran away from home—and still, nothing had changed.

"How many times have you been late paying your rent?" Greg pressed her.

"Three, maybe four times," she shrugged, not really sure. She paid it when she had it, and that was the best she could do. "But he—the landlord, that is—says he has a right to kick me out even though I've got two more years left on my lease."

"Did you bring your lease with you? Or the canceled checks to prove when you paid the rent?"

Gwen was shaking her head even as Greg spoke. "No. I didn't think to bring anything, except myself. Usually that's more than enough," she added with a hard little laugh that somehow touched Greg more than anything else had in months.

"Good, then you'll have to come back again soon and bring all that information with you."

Gwen looked over at him in surprise. "Do you really mean you're glad I have to come back. I mean, you want to see me again?" she spoke hesitantly, almost shyly.

Although Greg had said "good" without thinking, Gwen's surprise was so genuine that he couldn't bring himself to deflate her. "Of course I did. I want to get this business cleared up for you—and the sooner your landlord knows that you've got a lawyer working for you, the better."

"Oh." She sounded disappointed. "You were talking...strictly business."

Looking at her crestfallen face, Greg felt compelled to restore her confidence. In the office light her hair had appeared copper-colored, but now, under the power of the summer sun, it glowed like a flame. A flame-haired beauty, he thought, that's what Gwen Sherman could be if she only learned how to dress, style her hair, and apply makeup subtly.

"What about another picnic," he asked impulsively, "a real picnic with an empty meadow, a wicker basket full of goodies, and a bottle of wine?"

In answer, Gwen's smile glowed as brightly as her hair. "Do you mean it?"

"Scout's honor." Greg held up two fingers—and the funny thing was that he really found himself looking forward to Gwen's next visit.

***

Leslie Brooks appeared to have the world at her feet. To a girl like Gwen Sherman, her life looked as perfect as a fairy tale. Leslie had matured into a lovely, subtle-featured beauty. She had a wonderful family, exquisite clothes, and all the money she could ever want. Most exciting of all, she was on the threshold of a glorious career as a concert pianist, the dream she had cherished and worked for all her life. Her debut in Chicago had been hailed by the critics as the emergence of a major new talent on the musical scene, and now she was embarked on a five-city concert tour that would begin in Detroit and culminate with a piano recital at Carnegie Hall in New York City.

But as she packed her bags for the tour, Leslie felt as if her heart were breaking. None of the success, none of the acclaim she had always dreamed of meant anything now, because the center of her life was empty. In moments of blackest depression, Leslie wished that she had never met Brad Elliot. Until he came into her life, filling it with his brooding mystery and deep, penetrating passion, she had been content with nothing except her music. Now, though, no matter how urgently she played, or how thoroughly she immersed herself in her music, she felt hollow inside.

Instead of easing her sense of loss, time only seemed to intensify it. Life without Brad had no meaning, no joy. Her body ached from wanting him. What had she done wrong? How had she lost him?

Folding up the emerald silk stole she would wear on her opening night in Detroit and wrapping it carefully in tissue, Leslie searched her mind for answers, as she had done every day since Brad broke off their engagement almost five months ago. She'd planned a Christmas wedding with holly and white roses everywhere, and herself in a snow-white velvet gown. The dress still hung unused in a plastic bag in the back of her closet. At first Brad had suggested postponing the wedding, then, calling it off altogether. And Leslie loved him too much to beg him to change his mind, to plead with him to take a step he clearly wasn't ready for.

Although he insisted that he wanted to give her time and opportunity to establish her career as a concert pianist without the added pressures of marriage and a family, Leslie was sure that Brad was only trying to let her down gently. Hadn't her sister Laurie warned her that Brad was losing interest? A man as sensual and compelling as Brad Elliot was captivated by the challenge and conquest of winning a woman. But once victory was assured, his attention strayed— others appeared irresistibly attractive. When Leslie had insisted that Brad loved her, Laurie had laughed at her naïveté. Love meant sex to a man like Brad Elliot—and nothing more.

Laying the stole in her suitcase, Leslie tried to accept her sister's words, but her heart still rebelled. Brad *had* loved her, she told herself, needing desperately to cling to that belief, and maybe some part of him still did. If only she could find out! But she hadn't seen him once since the fateful night when he'd closed the door on her dream of marriage.

"Just about done packing, darling?" Jennifer Brooks asked brightly, coming into the room.

Leslie jumped at the sound of her mother's voice. She'd been so immersed in thoughts of Brad she hadn't heard Jennifer's knock. "Not quite," she admitted guiltily. It seemed as if she'd been packing for hours. But the trouble was she couldn't keep her mind on what she was doing. She kept forgetting what she needed to bring and what she'd already put in. As a result, she'd packed and unpacked a single bag three times.

"Come on, then. Let me give you a hand or you'll be at it till midnight. And you really do need your beauty sleep now. I don't think you have any idea how taxing a tour like this will be."

"I wish the whole thing were over," Leslie muttered bleakly.

"I didn't mean to sound negative, Les." Lovingly, Jennifer put her arm around her eldest daughter. "I know it will be wonderful... an unforgettable experience. Your father and I are so proud of you. I only wish we could be there with you in the front row at every single concert. But we'll try to get to as many of them as we can. And if we're not there in person, you know our hearts will be with you every moment."

"I don't want to go away, Mother," Leslie admitted. "I want to stay right here in Genoa City."

"Sounds to me as if you've come down with a first-class case of stage fright—which only makes you human like every other performer. I bet even Horowitz got a case of the jitters before each concert," Jennifer added as she began to fold her daughter's bathrobe.

"It's not that," Leslie said, flopping despondently down on the bed, grateful to leave the rest of the packing to her mother.

Jennifer paused in her work and studied her daughter intently. Leslie was even thinner than usual and the concert tour hadn't even begun yet. Her eyes were like huge dark hollows sunk in her pale, fragile face. Ever since she broke up with Brad Elliot Leslie had been despondent: picking at her food, closing herself off from the rest of the family, and submerging herself with frightening intensity in her music. Jennifer had watched and waited, hoping that in time Leslie would confide in her. Looking at her daughter now, though, she knew that she had to force the issue—no matter how reluctant Leslie was to discuss it.

"It's Brad Elliot that's still bothering you, isn't it? It has nothing to do with the concert tour," Jennifer said, resuming her packing with renewed vigor. When Leslie didn't answer, Jennifer knew she was right.

"What happened between you two, darling? It's been months and you've kept all your pain locked up inside you. Why don't you at least try to talk about it? Maybe it will help you. . .in any case it can't hurt," Jennifer coaxed.

"There's nothing to say," Leslie murmured.

"Why don't you begin by telling me why you broke up?"

Jennifer watched her daughter's narrow shoulders rise and fall in a hopeless shrug as she turned away. "Brad got tired of me," she spoke into the pillow.

"That's hard to believe, darling. Brad Elliot looked to me like a young man who was very much in love."

"Love doesn't mean anything—at least, not to

a man." Leslie's voice broke like glass shattering into a thousand tiny shards.

"Is that what Brad told you, Leslie?" Jennifer asked, going over to the bed. She sat down on the edge and stroked her daughter's hair comfortingly.

Even though Leslie had buried her head in the pillow, Jennifer could see it shake negatively. "What exactly did he tell you?" she persisted.

With an enormous struggle of will, Leslie brought her quavering voice under control. "He said I shouldn't think about marriage until after I get my career established. If we got married and I had to give up my music, I'd always regret it."

"And you didn't believe him?"

"I love him...I want to marry him—not a piano," she broke down and sobbed.

"But you didn't believe him?" Jennifer pressed her daughter to admit her deepest feelings.

"Oh, Mother, don't you see? Brad was just trying to let me down gently. He didn't want to hurt me—any more than he had to."

"That's what you decided in your own mind, Leslie," Jennifer said firmly. "That's not what Brad told you. If you really love someone, you have to trust in him and believe him, as well as love him. Love and trust are inseparable. You can't have one without the other."

Leslie's sobs had quieted as her mother spoke, and for a long moment the only sound was the rhythmic ticking of the alarm clock on the bedside table. "You mean you believe what Brad said, Mother...and you want me to believe it too?" Leslie murmured finally.

"I mean that you should give the man you love the benefit of the doubt. Maybe he was truly concerned with your happiness. But you'll never find out unless you give him a chance to prove it. Now that your career is starting, you should let Brad know."

"What would I say?" Leslie asked, as helpless as a child.

"Why not invite him to your opening night concert in Detroit? That way you can see for yourself," Jennifer suggested.

For the first time in months, Leslie actually smiled. "Do you really think I should, Mother?" she asked, excited by the idea yet still unsure, afraid to be hurt again. A second rejection now would be more than she could bear.

Jennifer got up, all business once again, ready to go back to the packing. "I only know one thing for sure, Leslie. You can never win anything or anyone unless you at least try." Although her voice was bright with confidence and conviction, in her heart Jennifer was saying a fervent prayer that Brad Elliot wouldn't hurt her daughter again.

In her mother's capable hands the packing was finished in no time and Leslie sat down at her desk to write to Brad, feeling more lighthearted and hopeful than she had in months. Maybe her mother was right and Laurie was wrong. Maybe Brad really was thinking only of her. Maybe he loved her so much, he was trying to put her happiness before his own. But how could he ever think that she could be happy without him? Leslie's mind was a jumble of thoughts, one wonderful "maybe" chasing after the other as she began to write:

"Dear Brad, You may have heard from Dad or Laurie that I'm starting out on a five-city concert tour tomorrow. I know this is short notice, but my first concert is in Detroit on Friday night and I would like you to be there. I hope you can come because I miss you and love you more than I can ever say. Love, Leslie."

Leslie was just licking the envelope to seal it when Laurie stuck her head in the door. "I saw that you were still up so I thought I'd pop in and say goodnight...and 'break a leg.' I may not see you in the morning. Dad said your flight was at dawn."

"Six-thirty, which is just as bad," Leslie laughed, suddenly feeling on top of the world. "Are you just getting home from the paper?"

"Late shift again," Laurie nodded.

"You should get Dad to give you better hours. You've been working late every night for weeks. You must feel like a zombie."

"Not quite," Laurie laughed slyly. "Actually, I never felt better, and you know that the publisher never plays favorites with his reporters... especially with the one who happens to be his daughter. Sometimes I think Dad makes me work twice as hard as anybody else on the *Genoa City Herald* just to prove how fair he is."

"You love being a reporter and you know it," Leslie said, "almost as much as I love my music."

"You don't hear me complaining, do you?" Laurie admitted. "Anyway, you're the one who should be in bed, instead of sitting up writing letters tonight of all nights. Who are you writing to, anyway?"

"Actually," Leslie admitted, feeling her cheeks

turn pink, "it's a letter to Brad."

"To Brad?" Laurie couldn't keep the surprise out of her voice. "I thought it was all over between you two months ago."

"It was...and maybe it still is," Leslie added, trying to sound sophisticated in front of her sister. "But I just thought I'd invite him to my first concert. He's been a good friend, and he always encouraged my music."

"And if he goes to your concert, you'll probably have dinner afterwards, champagne even, and one thing will lead to another, and who knows? You may be back in each other's arms again. Is that what you're thinking?" Laurie said sarcastically.

"Well, it's not impossible, after all," Leslie admitted, embarrassed to have her dreams spread out before her so coldly. "You think I'm being ridiculous, don't you?"

"Foolish, yes. Ridiculous?...I'm not Dear Abby, you know. Crazier things than that have happened," she added. Slipping into the room, she kissed Leslie lightly on the cheek and grabbed the letter from her hand. "Good luck, Sis. I'll personally deliver this to Mr. Bradley Elliot at the office tomorrow so he'll be sure to get it—and I'll even offer to work in his place Friday night, so he won't have any excuses."

"I can mail it on my way to the airport," Leslie offered tentatively.

"I wouldn't hear of it," Laurie insisted, waving good-night. "I'm much more reliable than the U.S. postal service."

Alone in her room, Laurie locked her door and tore open the letter. Leslie could wait until doomsday for Brad to show up at one of her concerts, because he would never see her insipid invitation. She'd had her chance to hook Brad, and she'd let him get away. Laurie wasn't about to make the same mistake. Ripping the letter into tiny pieces, she dropped it into an ashtray and carefully lit a match. This was one invitation that Brad Elliot would never R.S.V.P. Laurie had her own plans for him now. And there was no part in them for Leslie.

Chapter Two

Picnic in the Rain

The Elegance Beauty Salon, the choicest such shop Genoa City had to offer, had walls that were mirrored or painted mauve. In the morning coffee was served to customers in dainty flowered china cups; in the afternoon, tea with *petit fours*. And at all times of the day, while legs were being waxed, hair colored a more youthful shade, and wrinkles subjected to rigorous facials, the latest, hottest gossip of Genoa City was exchanged.

Although she closed her eyes, Jill Foster couldn't block out the lively tongues that washed over her like the garbled talk coming from the Tower of Babel.

"Poor Phil Chancellor," one hennaed matron was clucking to another, "I don't understand how he can stand it. They say Kay is drinking more than ever. In fact, she made quite a scene at the club the other night."

"I heard about it, and my husband says that Phil

has just washed his hands of her. He told her that he won't have a thing to do with her until she sobers up."

"Well, that should make Kay come to her senses, if anything will."

"Not Kay. She said 'the hell with you, Phil,' and from what I understand, she's taken up with the Chancellors' stableboy instead."

Jill shut her eyes tighter and tried to relax. But at seventeen it was hard not to be affected by the kind of malicious talk that swirled around her. Mrs. Chancellor did have a drinking problem, Jill thought, but why didn't any of these women who were supposed to be her friends try to help her, instead of spreading such malicious gossip all over town?

For two years, Jill had worked at the shop as a manicurist after school. When it was a part-time job, she'd managed to ignore the ceaseless, cruel gossip. But now that she had graduated and was working a full day, it was getting to her. And the stylists were no better than the customers. In fact, one egged on the other, salivating over each new tidbit. More than anything, Jill wanted to tell them all off and walk out. But after just two weeks on a full-time schedule, she knew she couldn't. Her mother and brothers had been working for years so that the Fosters could stay together as a family. And the added bonus of Jill's salary, small though it was, was sorely needed.

On the one hand, Jill hated being poor. But on the other, she never wanted to end up like the women she saw every day at the salon. Of course there were exceptions—like Jennifer Brooks, and even Kay Chancellor. For all her problems, Mrs.

Chancellor was superior to most of the other regular customers. She was much too imperious to ever stoop to petty, catty talk about her friends' private lives.

"Jill, your four o'clock appointment is at the desk," the receptionist's high, nasal twang called through the intercom.

Smoothing back her own dark hair, Jill quickly lined up the bottles of nail polish, arranging them in darkening hues from neutral to shell pink to burgundy red, and refilling the small hand basin with warm sudsy water. Praying that the two old women closest to her manicure table would find someone else to gossip about, she went out to the front to greet her appointment.

Kay Chancellor was drumming her long raspberry nails impatiently on the desk by the time Jill got there.

"My dear, I thought you'd forgotten I existed," she announced in her loud, throaty voice.

"I'm sorry if I kept you waiting," Jill apologized. "I only heard one call."

"It doesn't matter now, as long as you're ready for me." Kay Chancellor dismissed Jill's apology and the whole affair with a wave of her hand.

"Of course I'm ready, Mrs. Chancellor. You know you're one of my favorite customers."

"That's dear of you to say, Jill," she said sincerely, following the girl into the salon and dropping into the cushioned chair. "I mean it. I'm not the most popular person in town these days, as I'm sure you've heard from this gaggle of old biddies," she added, throwing her head back disdainfully to include all the other customers.

"I try not to listen to everything that's said," Jill

admitted, taking Mrs. Chancellor's ringed hand and placing it in the basin to soak while she removed the old polish from the other hand. "If I did, I don't think I'd be able to last here full time for very long."

"My dear," Mrs. Chancellor said, studying her intensely, "Why, I never stopped to think before, but, of course, you're absolutely right. A place like this is not the atmosphere for a sweet young thing like you to be exposed to day after day. Now if you were a tough old bird like me, you wouldn't give it a second thought. But you...how old are you, Jill?"

"Seventeen. I just graduated from high school a couple of weeks ago."

"I remember, and you were right up there at the top of your class, weren't you? It's a shame you can't go on to college. But maybe, someday..." She lifted her dripping hand out of the water for Jill to dry and massage with lotion.

"That's what my brothers say," Jill replied. "'Rambling Rose' today, Mrs. Chancellor?"

Kay Chancellor studied the nail polish bottle that Jill held up, but she wasn't thinking about the color. She was thinking about the girl. Her voice sounded so hopeless—as hopeless as Kay felt, despite every reason she had to be happy: a generous, loving husband, a son, a beautiful home, more money than she could ever spend... How much worse it must be for someone like Jill, with her whole life ahead of her and no prospects, no money, no future beyond the Elegance Salon.

"Rambling Rose?" Jill repeated.

Kay held out her hand in answer. She didn't

give a damn really what color her nail polish was as long as it wasn't an insipid pink. "I have a proposition for you, Jill," she said impulsively. "I don't know how you'll feel about it, but I need someone to give me a hand—a girl Friday, really, to keep the house running smoothly, plan the meals, answer invitations. . .that sort of thing. Of course, it would have to be someone I like and trust. That's why I thought of you. I probably couldn't pay you much more than you're making here at first, but in time. . ."

"Do you mean it, Mrs. Chancellor?" Jill stopped in the middle of her work, and a large drop of polish plopped like a puddle on Kay's index finger.

"Well, it's something for you to think about anyway, Jill, but obviously not now," she added, wagging her soiled finger to attract the girl's attention back to her work.

"I'm sorry, Mrs. Chancellor," Jill apologized profusely, grabbing a tissue and cleaning off the offending spot. "I don't know what to say. . ."

"Well, don't say anything right now," she advised tartly. "That way you can concentrate on finishing my manicure. You'll have plenty of time to think about it later and to talk it over with your family."

"Do you mind if I do?" Jill asked tentatively. Although she knew Kay Chancellor was a troubled woman, her offer of a job in her elegant home seemed like the answer to Jill's prayer.

"Mind? I insist that you do. You're still a very young woman, Jill, with a great deal to learn about the world. Get all the advice you can, my dear, and then make up your own mind. That way you have only yourself to blame if things don't work out the way you'd hoped." She waved her polished hands through the air to dry them. "I'm in no rush, Jill. When you've made your decision, call me. You have the number."

With her silver-white hair, her tall, still-slim figure, and her commanding manner, Kay Chancellor was very much a presence wherever she went. Although she appeared as imperious as a dowager empress, she could be very warm and generous to the people she liked—and quite clearly she had taken a liking to Jill Foster. Maybe she saw traces of herself reflected in the impressionable, young girl. Or maybe she felt sorry for the Fosters, who were struggling to survive on so little while she was free to sqaunder so much. Whatever her reason, Kay had offered Jill the opportunity of a lifetime. And, young as she was, Jill already knew better than to turn it down.

Although Greg had forgotten about his promise of a real picnic, Gwen hadn't, and she arrived at his office a week later with a wicker basket on her arm. As if she'd read his thoughts the previous time they were together, she was wearing a simple, pale blue sundress of gauzy cotton, sandals on her bare feet, and just the faintest brush of make-up. Her brilliant hair fell softly around her shoulders.

Perfect, Greg thought admiringly, almost as perfect as Chris. Although his day was already crowded, he felt like a heel for not remembering—especially when she had clearly observed so much about him. Even though it would mean working at the office long into the night, he made a few calls to rearrange his schedule while she sat in the chair beside his desk waiting as demurely as a schoolgirl. If she realized he had forgotten her, she never mentioned it—which only compounded his feelings of guilt.

Once in his car, driving out of town, with a summer breeze blowing back Gwen's hair, Greg told himself that he would make it up to her when they found a spot for their picnic. He knew just the place. Years before, his father had taken them there one summer Sunday. Looking back now, Greg realized that it was the last time his father had taken the family out. The next week he was gone.

Although they were only a few miles out of town, it looked as if they were deep in the country. On a distant crest of hill, beyond rolling green meadows where a herd of cows lolled indolently under the warming sun, stood a red-roofed barn and silo. It was just as Greg remembered it, unchanged in spite of the years that had passed. He pulled the car up onto the grassy shoulder and stared at the scene for a moment, letting the happy memories float over him, and wondering if Snapper and Jill remembered that long-ago afternoon as clearly as he did. Memories were so tricky. What one cherished, another recalled with boredom, even bitterness.

"This looks terrific," Gwen was saying eagerly, "like a picture in a storybook compared to my folks' farm. Back home it's all mud and dung and flies as big as chickens, especially at this time of year."

"You mean it, don't you?" Greg laughed. Grabbing the picnic basket, he got out and followed Gwen as she scrambled over the low wall as nimbly as a mountain goat. She really is a country girl, he thought, as they ran across the field to the shade of a silent pine grove.

"You open the wine while I set up the picnic," Gwen ordered, flopping down on the grass and spreading open the tablecloth. And Greg readily obeyed.

Uncorking the ice-cold bottle, he poured out two cups and lay back, his arms crossed under his head, watching Gwen. She looked almost like the girl he had envisioned in her cool sundress, busily arranging their lunch on the flowered paper tablecloth. Just beyond, wild flowers bloomed in random profusion—Queen Anne's lace and foxtails and delicate lilies-of-the-valley. A vine of fragrant honeysuckle wound around the thick trunk of an old red maple, filling the air with its intoxicating perfume. Overhead, fleecy clouds banked up in the blue sky.

It was hard for Greg to remember that they were supposed to be having a working lunch. The day, the setting, and Gwen herself seemed designed to make legal questions irrelevant.

"Did you bring the papers this time?" he asked, handing her a cup of wine.

She sat back on her heels and nodded. "Can't they wait until dessert, though?"

"I'll drink to that." He grinned and raised his cup to hers, feeling happier and more relaxed than he had in months. "What's for lunch, chef?"

"Fried chicken, potato salad, brownies, grapes, cheese."

"Think we'll have enough?" he teased.

Gwen laughed. "I hope you're hungry because I brought enough food for an army of lawyers."

"Can you imagine what that would be like? I mean an army of lawyers all nitpicking at every order. That would be one sure way to end war. There'd be so much talk—arguments, challenges, cross-examinations—no one would ever get to the battlefield."

Greg found himself talking easily to Gwen about his work and his family. Although she didn't make him feel as if she were prying, she seemed to ask the questions that would draw him out. Before they even got to the dessert, he had told her about his father and their last picnic, with the family in this very same meadow, and about his years at Yale Law School back east. He might have gone on talking if a sudden summer shower hadn't caught them unaware. More observant picnickers might have noticed that the cows in the meadow beyond had clustered together and sat down—a sure sign of rain, especially to a farm girl like Gwen. But she was too engrossed in Greg to notice anything else.

Lightning crackled suddenly. The fleecy clouds darkened and opened. Abandoning their picnic, the couple raced for cover into the dense grove of pines nearby. The thick green needles on the trees muffled the sound of the rain and offered an umbrella against the wetness. The ground under the trees was spread with thick layers of brown needles that had fallen over many a season and year.

Winded, Gwen sank down onto them as if they were a bed. Her sundress clung to her figure, the wetness making it almost transparent.

"You're soaked," Greg murmured, kneeling down beside her. The outline of her body was visible through the thin cotton, revealing clearly that she was wearing next to nothing under her dress.

"You should see yourself," she smiled, drops of rain shining on her long lashes.

"I'd rather see you."

Although they were alone, Greg whispered the words like a caress and heard his heart pounding from more than the race across the fields. For the first time, he didn't think of Chris. He didn't think of anyone or anything except the smiling girl holding out her hands to him. As Greg took them, Gwen lay back, drawing him down with her. Her flaming hair fanned out around her face, forming a shining frame for everything they did.

Gwen's lips reached up and drew his irresistibly to hers. Greg felt her soft young breath against his face. For so long he had denied himself all feeling, but now it was as if something inside had finally burst open, enabling him to connect with the parts he had repressed for what seemed like years. Gwen, in turn, seemed to welcome him, as if to assure him that she understood, and it was all right.

Greg never had to hesitate, never had to wonder if she would let him take the next step, because Gwen led him subtly yet surely, like a guide charting a path through unexplored territory. Her body was like a precision instrument, and she used it knowingly to fire him with a tumultuous need. It was as though she knew instinctively how to arouse his body so that every nerve end crackled with desire.

The rain stopped as suddenly as it started, and the sun began to shine brightly again. In the distance the cows mooed contentedly. They lay side by side, with only their fingertips touching, staring up into the canopy of damp needles.

"We should be getting back. I've kept you from your office too long already," Gwen said softly.

"Not long enough," Greg replied, wishing the rain had gone on and on. "When can I see you again?"

"For another legal consultation?" she teased.

Gwen had seemed so hard at their first meeting, and now she seemed so vulnerable and defenseless. "For anything you want," he promised.

"And anything *you* want you can have," she answered, adding mischievously—"scout's honor."

Chapter Three

Unanswered Dreams

The darkened concert hall spread in front of her like a half-moon, hushed and expectant, as the single spotlight followed the slender young girl gliding out from the wings. Leslie's gown fanned behind her in a full train as she floated ethereally across the stage and took her place at the gleaming grand piano. For a moment she sat, her hands poised in high, rounded arcs over the ivory keys, trying to compose herself. But her heart was beating so fast and hard she was afraid the audience could hear it. It wasn't stage fright that set it thumping, but the thought, the hope, that out there in the sea of waiting faces was one special one—the one she would play her very best for tonight.

Brad hadn't accepted Leslie's invitation. But neither had he declined it—and slim though it was, that hope gave Leslie something to hold fast to, something to carry her through the opening night concert in Detroit. Her eyes shining brighter than the stage lights that illumined her, she took a deep breath and began to play a Beethoven sonata. She gave herself up to the music, pouring out all her love, her deepest feelings, her excitement, her most cherished dreams, because she was playing for the man she loved.

The audience rewarded her with thunderous applause. But that was just a prelude. The more Leslie played, the more totally she surrendered to the music and to the passion that welled in her heart. By the time she reached the end of her program, she felt as if she had bared her soul for Brad, her music speaking more eloquently than any words she could say.

What would his answer be? Leslie wondered, as she rose slowly, like someone in a dream, to take her bow. Tendrils of dark curls clung to her moist forehead as she turned to face the audience. It was only then that she realized the symphony hall was silent—so silent her heels clicked like castanets as she crossed the stage. Panic seized her. What had she done wrong? Had the rest of the audience felt excluded from her performance? She'd been playing so intensely for Brad, she had completely forgotten that hundreds of others had been listening too. Leslie's eyes darted nervously over the vast sea before her, but the bright lights blinded her so that she couldn't see clearly.

Curtsying hastily, she had already started to turn toward the wings when the first wave of applause broke over her. The audience had been stunned by the raw power of her performance. Now it found its voice. Once the applause started, it was like an avalanche sweeping over her. Flowers rained onto the stage. Shouts of "bravo!" and "encore!" resounded through the hall. Distinguished men and women were standing at their seats, cheering the fragile young unknown whom they had been privileged to discover that night. From the wings, the stage manager pushed Leslie back to take yet another bow, whispering under his breath for her to play an encore.

As if in a dream, Leslie took her place again at the piano bench and began to play—not another classical piece, but American originals from Porgy and Bess. The audience loved it and insisted on more.

By the time she finished her fourth encore, she was too exhausted to continue. Trembling yet triumphant, she blew a final kiss to her exultant new fans and stepped back to let the curtain fall. The night belonged to her—and to Brad. He was out there—he had to be. She could never have played like that if she didn't believe that Brad had been listening, that he could hear the cry of her heart in every note.

Alone in her dressing room, Leslie waited with mounting excitement for the knock that she was sure would be his. The tiny mirrored room was banked with flowers from the maestro, Chris and Snapper, her parents, and friends from Genoa City. There was even a little old-fashioned bouquet of rosebuds centered in a lace-like paper doily and tied with streamers of pink ribbon from her sister Peggy. The largest arrangement, though, was a wreath of carnations and gladiola, so big it could have been a funeral piece, from her sister Laurie. Leslie read each card with tears in her eyes, thinking the next one would be from Brad. Even when she reached the last, though, she wouldn't let herself be disappointed. Brad didn't need to send flowers when he was sending himself. Any moment he would walk through the dressing room door and take her in his arms. Although it was a dream, she believed it with her whole heart and soul.

"Darling, you were a sensation!" Jennifer burst into the room with Peggy pushing excitedly behind her and hugged Leslie, her cheeks glowing with pride. "You should hear the talk out there. Everyone is saying, 'Leslie Brooks is the new Van Cliburn.' I wish your father could have been here. He would have exploded with pride."

"Was there anyone else out there you knew?" Leslie asked tensely, the first tremor of fear shaking her voice.

Jennifer, knowing the answer to her question yet not wanting to give it, hugged her tighter and then released her. "Aren't you excited, darling?" she asked brightly. "You looked like a queen out there, and you played like an angel."

"Of course I'm excited. I just thought maybe you'd seen somebody we know." Although Leslie tried to sound casual, Peggy wasn't fooled any more than her mother was.

"Leslie means Brad Elliot, I bet, Mom," she piped up with all the tact of a typical teenager.

"No, darling, we didn't see any *old* fans, but you made hundreds of new ones here tonight," Jennifer said, praying that the excitement of Leslie's debut would cushion her disappointment.

"I invited Brad, like you said." Leslie sank down

on the dressing table stool, her voice suddenly soft and tremulous.

"He probably couldn't get away," Jennifer said, making the excuse to comfort her daughter, not because she believed it. "I'm sure Brad would have told your father if he were planning to come. But don't worry, darling, you'll give lots more concerts that Brad can hear. I'm no music critic, but after tonight I bet you'll need a full-time manager just to answer all the requests you'll be getting for concerts and recitals and guest appearances. You won't have any time to wonder who's out there in the audience."

Although Leslie tried to listen to her mother, tried to let herself be carried away by Jennifer's enthusiasm, her heart felt as if it were shattering again. She knew she would never play as well as she had tonight. Every other concert would be a disappointment because the music she made would sound as hollow as she felt.

Maybe it would have been better if Leslie had cried, instead of holding back the terrible sorrow that was devouring her inside. But she couldn't cry. It was as if everything within her—her aspirations, her hopes, her dreams, her joy, even her tears—had been consumed.

"There'll be other concerts, darling," Jennifer was saying. "So many others. I'm sure Brad will be able to hear you before your tour is over, if that's what you want so much. But tonight you should be happy. We'll have a champagne supper at the best restaurant in town—and we won't let anything spoil such a triumphant debut. What do you say, Leslie?"

"Oh, Les, you've got to say yes," Peggy chimed

in excitedly. "I bet everybody will recognize you and want your autograph... just like a real star, a theatrical celebrity or someone. Do you have a pen? I brought one along," she said, fishing in her purse and producing a red ball-point pen, "just in case."

Leslie knew she couldn't disappoint Peggy or her mother, no matter how much she was hurting. They were both so proud and excited. "Of course we'll celebrate, Peg—all night long if you like," she added, forcing a smile on her tight lips.

"Then come on! What are we waiting for?" Jennifer called with forced gaiety. She wished her husband had been able to attend the concert— and not just so that he could savor Leslie's triumph. Stuart Brooks had always enjoyed a special closeness with his eldest daughter, although they had little in common. He was confident, aggressive, always out in front on every issue. It was what made him such an intrepid newspaper publisher. By comparison, Leslie was sensitive, quiet, and painfully shy. Maybe it was because they were opposite in temperament that Stuart was so tender and protective with Leslie—always encouraging her, yet never pushing her too hard. It was a fine line, and he had held to it mindfully through the years of Leslie's adolescence. With his other daughters he seemed to make unforgivable mistakes. But where Leslie was concerned, his instincts rarely failed him.

Damn the newspaper! Jennifer thought angrily, and damn its ace reporter, Bradley Elliot! Nothing was more important than Leslie's happiness. Tonight she should be floating on air. Instead, she was sinking into a dangerous depression.

Jennifer wasn't deceived by Leslie's attempt at gaiety, even though Peggy was. Had she been wrong to suggest sending an invitation to Brad? Had she raised her daughter's hopes only to see them dashed again—even more cruelly this time? All through the winter Jennifer had been so concerned about Chris's suffering a miscarriage and separating from her husband that she didn't have time to worry about Leslie's breakup with Brad. Now Jennifer wished she'd been more sympathetic. Maybe she could have helped Leslie to forget Brad and start again with someone new, someone who would be better for her. Brad was so mysterious, so secretive about himself, that Jennifer had actually been relieved when he had called off the wedding.

Now, though, Chris and her husband were back together and it was Leslie whose heart seemed permanently damaged. Jennifer was sick with worry about her oldest daughter. Alone on the road, following the grueling tour schedule, staying in lonely hotel rooms with no family to support her, no comforts of home to ease the pain, Leslie might never be able to recover.

Jill Foster's mouth dropped open as she stepped across the threshold of the Chancellors' house for the first time. The place looked as though it had been cut out of the glossy color pages of *House Beautiful*. No one can possibly live like this, she thought, gazing around the square foyer with its gleaming black-and-white marble floor to the long, elegant living room beyond. A maid in a black uniform and starched white apron waited to announce her.

"Who shall I say is calling?" the woman asked, prodding Jill out of her reverie.

"Jill. Jill Foster." Her name came out in a small, little-girl voice, and she cleared her throat self-consciously.

"And who are you here to see, Miss Foster?"

"Actually," Jill stammered, awe-struck by the surroundings and by the maid who seemed impatient with her, "I'm not really here to see anyone. I'm going to be working for Mrs. Chancellor. This is my first day."

"Then you came to the wrong entrance." The maid cut off her explanation. "You should have used the servants' door around to the side."

"Well, I'm not really a servant," Jill answered, glad that her brother Snapper wasn't there to overhear the maid's remark.

Snapper had been opposed to her taking the job at the Chancellors for that very reason. He didn't want anyone in Genoa City getting the idea that his sister was a servant. No matter how much Jill hated the Elegance Salon, being a manicurist was better than being somebody's maid, he said. In the end, though, after realizing that she was going to be more like a private secretary than a domestic, Snapper had relented in spite of his misgivings. Now Jill felt obliged to correct the maid's mistake so that Snapper would let her stay. Ever since their father had walked out on them, Snapper had made all the major family decisions. And even though he was married, he still acted like the head of the Foster house.

"Mrs. Chancellor said I was going to be her girl Friday," Jill explained eagerly. But the unyielding expression on the maid's face made her add, "That's something like a secretary, I think."

"You can call it anything you like, but if you work for the Chancellors you use the other door, understand?" she said stubbornly. "If you're not a Chancellor or a guest of the Chancellors, then you're not one of *them*. You're one of *us*. Same goes for all the others—gardeners, cooks, stableboys..."

"I'd like to be one of them," Jill blurted out, "and live in this beautiful house. It's like a palace."

"Who wouldn't?" the maid laughed. "Anyway," she said, softening a little, "since you're here now, you might as well stay."

"Thanks," Jill said, grateful that she could go home and tell Snapper that she had marched right in the front door. "Do you really have a stable and stableboys?" she asked incredulously.

"Sure do. Who else would take care of the horses? They're Mr. Chancellor's pride and joy— the only things in the whole place that don't disappoint him, if you ask me," she added cryptically.

"What's he like? Mr. Chancellor, I mean?" Jill inquired curiously.

"The exact opposite of her. He's the kindest gentleman you could ever meet." As she spoke the maid shook her head, as if she didn't approve of much of anything except Phillip Chancellor.

"What's going on out there, Emma? Whom are you talking to?" a rich, modulated voice called out. Then a face peered through the dining room door, fixing Jill with frank, amused eyes.

"Whom have you come to see? My son Brock—and so early in the morning?"

Phillip Chancellor stood just over six feet. Strong, sculpted features were emphasized by thick black hair and a full mustache. Although he was dressed in a tailor-made navy pinstripe suit, Jill could imagine him astride a powerful horse, galloping over a green meadow. Smile lines softened his face, giving it an almost boyish glow.

Jill found herself smiling back. "No, sir. I've never met your son. Mrs. Chancellor asked me to be her girl Friday. This is my first day."

Jill thought she saw Phillip Chancellor's face darken at the mention of his wife, but it may have been a shadow crossing instead.

"May I ask where my wife found you?" he inquired sharply.

"I was manicuring her nails. She was one of my regular customers at the Elegance Beauty Salon downtown where I worked... and when I told her how much I hated my job, she offered to hire me. Can you imagine?"

"All too well, my dear," Phillip Chancellor sighed. "I wonder what state my wife was in when she made that little proposition..." he began, then stopped himself abruptly. "What's the difference? The fact is you're here, and you've probably already given up your job at the beauty parlor, haven't you?"

Jill nodded bleakly. "I'm afraid I have. I hated it so..."

"Well, what did you say your name was?"

"Jill Foster."

"Well, Jill, it's out of the frying pan and into the

fire. Come on in and have some breakfast, and you can tell me all you know about being a girl Friday. There's no point in calling my wife yet. She hasn't made an appearance downstairs before noon in five years."

"Never say never, Phil darling!" a husky voice interrupted before Jill could reply.

"Are you just going to bed, or are you actually sober enough to get up in the morning?" Phillip asked acidly, his tone as sharp as vinegar. He barely glanced up the stairwell to where his wife was poised precariously on the second-floor railing.

"If you were more of a husband, you wouldn't have to ask," Kay shot back, leaning further over the bannister.

Looking up, Jill caught her breath. Another inch or two and her new employer would topple over the rail and splatter at her feet. "Be careful, Mrs. Chancellor," she gasped.

"Don't worry, Jill," Phillip answered bitterly. "My wife's much too drunk ever to fall—unless of course I push her, which I must confess I'm tempted to do from time to time. But enough of our sordid family history. If you decide to stick it out here—and I warn you, it won't be a picnic— you'll find out plenty on your own, without my help." He turned back into the dining room, as if he'd forgotten his wife was literally hanging over them, and motioned Jill to join him.

The girl hesitated, her loyalties between the two Chancellors tested for the first time. Then she glanced up again. The apparition of Kay Chancellor had disappeared from the stairway, so she followed Phillip dutifully into the dining room. Was he being cruel? Or was the gossip that had circulated so freely in the Elegance Salon more accurate than Jill had believed? Jill's life, for all its hardships, had been a sheltered one. Although she knew Kay Chancellor had a drinking problem, she had no idea what that meant in practical day-to-day terms, or how it could destroy even the most fortunate of families.

"How old are you, Jill?" Phil asked, indicating that she should sit opposite him in what was clearly his wife's place.

"I just turned eighteen," she answered proudly as she sat down. The oval table was cherry wood, highly polished and set with pale blue linen placemats and matching napkins. The china was white and dotted with tiny blue forget-me-nots. A Steuben Glass bowl of yellow marguerites sat in the center of the table.

"Eighteen," Phil said thoughtfully, ringing the matching china bell by his plate.

As if she'd been waiting by the door, another, older woman in a black maid's uniform and white apron came bustling in.

"This is Miss Foster, Maggie, and she's dying to sample one of your very special breakfasts. She's heard they're the best to be found anywhere in Genoa City," he said with a smile.

Although she'd received the same compliment many times, the old woman chuckled with delight, and came back a few minutes later bearing a covered silver platter of scrambled eggs and sausages. A basket filled with homemade biscuits followed and a pot of strong steaming coffee. It was a true feast—the kind of special breakfast that the Fosters only had at Christmas and Easter.

Jill couldn't resist and she piled her plate high, smearing sweet butter over the piping hot buttermilk biscuits.

Across the table, Phil Chancellor smiled broadly as he watched her. "I bet you dashed out of the house so fast this morning you only had time to grab a glass of juice."

"That's right," Jill began to say, her mouth full of sausages and eggs. Then, remembering her manners, she nodded vigorously instead.

"I suppose you need this job," he went on, "so there's no point in my telling you all the reasons why you'd be better off to forget all about it and go back home to your mother."

"My mother's not home—she works too," Jill said, swallowing just in time.

"Of course. How stupid of me," Phil said, as much to himself as to Jill. "Well, it looks like you're going to have to make the best of a bad situation—at least until we can find some other place for you."

"But I don't want some other place," Jill insisted, her wide eyes sweeping around the formal dining room. "Spending every day in a beautiful house like this is like living in a palace. I think I'm probably the luckiest girl in Genoa City, thanks to Mrs. Chancellor."

"Thanks to Mrs Chancellor," he repeated grimly, "you are going to learn things that no naïve young eighteen-year-old should be exposed to. Although this is a very beautiful house, Jill, it is not a happy one. My wife was once a strong, fine woman. Now she is a sick woman—

a very sick woman—but she refuses to accept help from anyone. Maybe with your youth and innocence you'll be able to do something for her that none of the rest of us has succeeded in doing. I sincerely hope so. But I think it's only fair to warn you that the elegant appearance of this place, which has obviously captured your imagination, is only skin-deep. Scratch that perfect surface and you'll discover misery, deception, and bitterness. A tall order for a girl like you." He paused and looked at her steadily until Jill was sure that his hazel eyes had pierced right through to her heart. "If you want to back out now, I'll give you two weeks pay and explain your decision to my wife. Selfishly, I'd like you to stay. It would be refreshing to have a bright, young face around here for a while, but you have to make your own decision. Either way, there'll be no hard feelings."

The breakfast, which had looked so tempting when Maggie served it, had lost much of its flavor while Phillip Chancellor talked. Jill played with her food nervously. With her barbed wit and regal manner, Kay Chancellor had always been one of Jill's favorite customers. It was hard for her to reconcile that commanding yet kind person with the one Phillip Chancellor had just described. And yet she couldn't believe that any man would invent such terrible lies about his own wife. Kay's sarcastic words, hurled down the stairwell at her husband, came back. "If you were more of a husband. . ." What did she mean? What private battle was being waged between Phillip and Kay Chancellor?

Jill looked across the table at Phillip Chancellor,

hoping to find some kind of answer in his eyes. But if there was a messge in them, she couldn't read it.

"Have you made up your mind, Jill?" he asked, holding her with his steady gaze.

"Mrs. Chancellor is expecting me. I gave her my word," Jill said, hoping that she sounded surer than she felt. "I can't very well back down now without even giving it a try."

"There aren't many people as good as their word. I hope you never change." He pushed his chair back and stood up. "Good luck, Jill," he said lightly, as if, now that his warning had been given, he was never going to refer to it again. "If I were you, I'd spend the rest of the morning roaming around. Go for a ride or something— get to know the place. Kay never likes to be disturbed before twelve or one o'clock."

"Thank you, sir," Jill murmured gratefully. but as she watched him walk out the door, she was filled with fear, as if she'd entered a magical kingdom and found it inhabited by unknown monsters. "Mr. Chancellor..." she called, suddenly afraid to be left alone.

"I hope I didn't spoil your appetite for breakfast," he said, turning back. "Maggie will be very insulted if she thinks you don't like it."

"Oh, no, it's not the breakfast," Jill answered quickly. "It's just that..." Her voice trailed off. "I was hoping we could talk a little more," she finished weakly.

A gentle smile softened his face, and he started toward her as if he were going to reach out and touch her; then he drew back. If she knew how to dress, how to do her hair, he thought, she could be quite striking, with her huge brown eyes and lustrous dark hair. Looking at her, he was filled with a gnawing ache. It had been so long since he'd known any woman except the ones whose services he discreetly paid for—willing girls who provided him a much-needed outlet, but no lasting satisfaction.

"I'll try to come home early to see how you're doing. Is that what you want?" he asked.

"Do you think you could?" she burst out, surprised by the wave of relief that swept over her at his words.

"I'm not promising," he smiled again. "But I'll do my best. I didn't mean to frighten you, Jill," he added apologetically. "You sound as if you have enough pluck to tough out any situation—even this one. It's an admirable quality...I hope you never lose it."

For the second time Jill watched him start out the door, and for the second time she stopped him. "Mr. Chancellor," she called again, "thank you."

He turned back just in time to catch her words. She looked lost, he thought, sitting alone at the big oval table surrounded by silver platters and a coffee service. Kay would have looked completely at ease, as if she were born there; but Jill looked like an abandoned child, and his heart went out to her.

"Take care of Kay," he murmured huskily, as if he were reluctant to leave her. Then he quickly turned away and went out.

Chapter Four

An Indecent Proposal

Stuart Brooks was both a newspaper publisher and a proud father, two very different occupations which he had never thought would conflict—until Leslie set out on her first concert tour. He didn't approve of promoting his own family within the pages of the *Genoa Herald*. On the other hand, he saw no reason why Leslie should be penalized simply because she was his daughter. If any other local girl were making her national debut as a concert pianist, he would have a reporter and photographer parked on her doorstep to do a feature story on the event. Why should Leslie get less attention?

The solution to his dilemma appeared in the evening edition the day Leslie's tour opened in Detroit. Underneath a four-column photograph of her seated at her own piano was a story bearing the publisher's personal byline. Usually Stuart Brooks only signed an editorial on controversial political subjects. But Leslie was an exception to every rule.

Seated alone at a back booth in the bar across the street from the newspaper office, Brad Elliot opened the paper to the publisher's story. He had purposefully waited until he could be alone to look at it, not trusting his self-control in the presence of strangers. Under the headline, "GENOA CITY PIANIST STARTS NATIONAL TOUR," he stared at the photograph of Leslie: her slender body bent over the piano keys; her fragile face, partly shadowed, intent on the music she was playing. It was a pose Brad had seen her in so many times before that it made his heart ache. She looked so involved, so totally absorbed in her music, that it seemed as if he must be far from her thoughts. Sadly, he traced her fine profile for the last time. The shadows hid the anguish, the pain, the desolation that etched her face. Until now, Brad had clung to a glimmer of hope that Leslie would come back to him. The truth weighed on him like a cold, leaden rock he could never lift. Leslie was gone from his life forever. Once he had given her the chance, she had soared free of him like some glorious bird; now she was embarked on a brilliant career that would lead her further and further away from his waiting arms. Laurie had been right about her sister, Brad thought, trying not to let his sorrow turn to bitterness. Leslie had a dream, and marriage would have only stood in the way of it—and ultimately destroyed it.

With a bleak sense of fatality, Brad wrenched his eyes from the girl he would always love and began to read the story her father had written about her:

"In the twenty years that I have served as publisher of this newspaper, I have tried to present every story with objectivity and detachment. For the first time, though, I have come upon a story which deserves to be told in these pages, but one about which I can claim neither objectivity nor detachment. It is the story of a lovely, dedicated young Genoa City girl who is making her debut tonight in Symphony Hall in Detroit, the first stop in an exciting five-city national tour that will culminate at Carnegie Hall in New York.

"Genoa City deserves to be proud of her. But no one could be prouder than I am. Because the promising young pianist in question is my own oldest daughter, Leslie Brooks..."

"I thought I'd find you here!"

Brad looked up, a lump in his throat, and found himself faced with Laurie Brooks's bright, brittle smile. "I was just reading about your sister," he said bleakly. "Quite an article your father wrote."

"It was tough for him," Laurie admitted, seating herself down beside Brad. "I think Dad sweated more over that story than any he's written in his entire life. I wonder what you would have written, if he'd given you the assignment." she added, eying him curiously.

"I would have asked to be reassigned," Brad answered with quick, sure conviction, "on the grounds of personal, insurmountable bias."

"Even now?" she asked, moving closer to him.

Brad nodded. "I don't think some things ever change."

"Meaning the way you feel about Leslie?"

"What do you think?"

"I think you should stop feeling so sorry for yourself. If you read Dad's article, you'd know that you did the right thing. Tonight Leslie will be doing what she's always dreamed of—and all because you were noble enough to give her the chance. Years from now, you'll look back and be happy for her...and happy for yourself."

"I hope you're right, Laurie," Brad said fervently, "because right now happy is the last thing I feel. I don't know why you've stood by me all these miserable months. I certainly haven't been very good company."

"Let's just say I have a vested interest in you," she acknowledged cryptically. "And besides, there's no one in Genoa City I'd rather be with, even when you're miserable."

"I don't know how I'll ever be able to repay you."

"Well, why don't you begin by taking me home to your place? I just happened to stop off at the market before I came here, and I have veal, rice, salad, fresh asparagus—all the fixings to make you an unforgettable dinner. There's a recipe I learned in Paris," she laughed. "Once you taste it, you forget all your troubles. It's supposed to be more foolproof than an aphrodisiac. And just in case it's not quite all it's chalked up to be, I picked up a couple of bottles of Chablis to get you in the mood."

Brad hesitated, remembering with embarrassment the last time he'd let Laurie take him home. He'd been so drunk and so depressed about losing Leslie that he'd behaved like an animal, pretending Laurie was her sister and doing

everything short of taking her into his bed. "Are
you sure you trust me, after last time?" he asked
uncertainly.

"Of course not," Laurie laughed suggestively
and took Brad's hand, pulling him up with her. "I
wouldn't waste my time on a man I could trust.
Boring."

"I don't know about you Parisian girls." Brad
found himself laughing, too. "You're too much
for me to understand."

"Then don't try," she countered. "Just enjoy
us."

An hour later they were snugly ensconced in
Brad's bachelor apartment. Brad was stretched
out on the sofa, a chilled glass of white wine on
the table beside him, drinking in the intoxicating
fragrance of simmering herbs.

"What do you say? Are you getting hungry?"
Laurie came to the kitchen door, her face flushed
from her cooking and from anticipation.

"If it tastes as good as it smells," Brad said,
opening his eyes, "it may be just as irresistible as
you said."

"Do you mean that?" Laurie asked softly,
crossing the room toward him. In the dim light
her suede skirt and sweater clung seductively to
the rounded curves of her body, and the
suggestive way she walked served to heighten
the effect.

Brad began to sit up, knowing that they were
moving into dangerous territory. It had been
months since he'd had a woman—not since he
and Leslie had broken up—and his body was
tense with the strain of denial. He'd been

waiting, holding himself back... in the hope that she would come back to him. Now his last shred of hope was dashed. Leslie was miles away, beginning a new life—a life in which he had no part.

"I have a little taste for you," Laurie was saying, "to whet your appetite, so to speak."

She reached the couch while Brad was still trying to sit up and, kneeling beside it, she pushed him back down. "I thought you'd at least get comfortable while I was in the kitchen," she murmured, reaching up to loosen his tie. "You don't have to stand on formalities with me, you know," she went on, her fingers quick at the buttons of his shirt. "There," she smiled, opening it and allowing her hands to roam over his bare chest, kneading the strong, tight muscles. "You were so tense. Doesn't that feel better?"

"Much," he admitted, inhaling sharply. Laurie's touch was like fire in a drought-stricken forest. "But don't you have to get back to the kitchen?"

"I turned everything on low," she murmured. "It was so hot in there, I had to escape for a minute. I wish I could take this sweater off," she sighed, raising it up as she spoke.

"Laurie, I don't think..." Brad began sharply. But either it was too late or she chose not to hear him, for she'd already lifted it over her head. She stretched like a cat, then, taking Brad's hands, pressed them against her pulsating body.

"Ummm," she sighed, "that feels much better than a sweater."

"Laurie, what are you doing?" he murmured hoarsely.

"Don't think, just let yourself feel," she promised him, "and you'll never want to stop." As she spoke her hands reached out for him. She wanted to claim him as her own, excite him, drive him beyond the limits of refusal.

Brad knew he should stop. She was Leslie's sister, after all, and yet that only seemed to drive him on. He could never have Leslie now. She was gone from his life forever, and Laurie was so willing, so eager, so ready for him.

"Brad," Laurie whispered triumphantly afterwards. "I told you I could make you forget Leslie if you only gave me the chance..."

Brad closed his eyes, trying to wipe away the picture of what he had just done, but now that she had finally gained a sure advantage, Laurie wasn't going to give it up.

"Well?" she demanded. "Did you like that, Brad?" Laurie pressed him, anxious to hear him admit that she was better than Leslie had ever dreamed of. Leslie was so naïve, so inexperienced, Laurie couldn't imagine that she was any good at making love.

He nodded, his eyes still shut tight, knowing that it was pointless to lie now, on top of everything else that he had just done. Laurie wouldn't be fooled anyway. Leslie had been a virgin when they made love the first time, but Laurie clearly knew how to pleasure a man. "We shouldn't have, Laurie," he groaned, tormented by his own guilt. What kind of man would make love to two sisters?

"Why not? We're both consenting adults... and we both enjoyed it," Laurie argued persuasively.

"Yes, but you're Leslie's sister." He ground out the words through clenched teeth, keenly aware that she had not yet exhausted her ability to excite him.

"Leslie is finished, Brad. I thought you realized that tonight," Laurie said, more sharply than she'd intended. "She has a new life, a career, other priorities—and so should you."

"It's not that easy," he admitted sadly. "I've been hoping that given time, Leslie would. . ."

"Don't you think that if Leslie still wanted you to be part of her life she would have invited you to her concert tonight?" Laurie asked, cutting him off abruptly.

"Actually, I kind of thought she might," Brad murmured. "I guess she was too busy."

"Busy!" Laurie scoffed. "She didn't invite you because you belong to an old life, and she's starting out on a new one. There's no place for you in it. What would you be? A classical groupie, following her around from city to city? Be realistic. You're holding on to a dream that's never going to happen. But this is real, Brad, the desire you're feeling right now—for me. It isn't Leslie you're holding in your arms now. I'm here with you because I want to be here. What's past is past. Over. Finished. But you and I are just beginning."

"Damn you, Laurie," he swore, pulling her down on him and bruising her lips with a savage kiss. It was true, every word she had said. He'd been waiting for an invitation from Leslie. It would have been the sign he was hoping for that they could still have a life together, no matter how successful she became. Instead, he had to accept the bitter truth that it was over between them. He had done the noble thing—and had lost her forever. And now there was Laurie Brooks, her sister. It could have been anyone. Any warm, willing body to drown his sorrow in.

Brad only wanted to forget—to lose himself, his memories, and his miseries in the frenzy he was allowing himself to feel. The more his heart cried out for Leslie, the more fiercely his emotions churned. He was oblivious to Laurie's feelings, to the deep welts her nails were scratching in his back and the sharp cut of her teeth in his shoulder.

"Brad, Brad..." she murmured again and again.

Through a haze of spent passion and failed dreams, he saw her. Tears glistened in her eyes like sunbeams on a pond, filling him with an even greater remorse.

"I hurt you," he said, blaming himself for everything that had gone so wrong. "I'm sorry, Laurie. You didn't deserve it. You were only trying to help me all through these months and now look how I've gone and repaid you!"

Laurie blinked her eyes to bring the tears spilling down her cheeks. "Why were you so cruel?" she managed to sob.

"I don't know," he said remorsefully. "I couldn't stop myself. But I'll make it up to you. I promise I will. I'll do anything you want, Laurie."

For a long moment she stroked his cheek, wondering if she were moving too fast. Then, deciding to seize the opportunity before it slipped away again, she said quietly, "There's only one thing I want, Brad. And that's to marry you."

"Marry me?" he repeated incredulously.

"Leslie is gone, Brad," she rushed on, "but I'm here, and I want you. You want me too, you know you do. You just proved it with your body, no matter what your mind may be thinking."

" "Is that really what you want, Laurie—even after what I just did to you?" he asked, stunned by her proposal.

"It's the only thing that will make what you just did all right. The only thing that could," she faltered, forcing fresh tears into her eyes, "that could make it not a rape."

The harshness of her accusation shocked him, and yet he couldn't deny the charge. He hadn't waited to find out if she wanted him again. Instead, he had forced himself on her, taking her violently, never pausing to consider her desires. A rush of memories swept over him. He thought of Barbara Anderson, the lusty nurse in Chicago who had loved him faithfully for so many years and begged him again and again to marry her. Instead, he had broken her heart. Then there was Leslie whom he wanted, still wanted, would always want—and never could have. Now there was Laurie, asking to take her sister's place. Asking him to prove that he hadn't used and abused her. She was asking for the self-respect he had brutally stripped from her. How could he deny her.

"I can't promise I'll be a good husband to you, Laurie," he warned, not caring whom he married if it couldn't be Leslie.

"I'm only asking for one promise at a time, Brad," she said shrewdly. "That's enough for any man to make."

"Then, if you're sure it's what you want..."
Her lips reached up to claim his. "I'm sure,
Brad," she murmured. "I've never been surer of
anything in my life."

Chapter Five

Unexpected Engagements

The unexpected rain that had interrupted Gwen's picnic had a more lasting effect on Greg than the usual summer shower. It opened his heart, which had been closed so tightly since Chris went back to his brother, Snapper. Often, in the weeks that followed, he found himself dreaming of flaming hair instead of strawberry blonde and looking forward to the next time he would see Gwen. What had started out as strictly a legal business, became more and more a personal one, until one day Greg realized that if it were up to him, Gwen's problems with her landlord would be over abruptly. Granted that it wasn't a legal solution, but it was an intensely satisfying one—if only he could get Gwen to agree.

"What are you thinking about?" she asked, reaching over to grasp his hand. They were having a drink at a cozy little cafe' down the street from the legal aid office, which had quickly become their special place. Greg would have liked to take Gwen out more often in the evenings. But she was usually busy. It seemed to Greg that she logged more overtime hours in her job as a clerk-typist than did the presidents of major companies. Six out of seven nights, when he asked her for a date, she said she was working late and would be too tired to see him by the time she got home. Instead, she managed to sneak away for a few hours in the afternoons to be with him. And when he commented on the uniqueness of her work schedule, she just laughed it off, blaming the eccentricity of her employer.

When she was with him, though, she seemed so happy that he was sure she wasn't deceiving him. Entwining his fingers through hers, he smiled at her, wondering if he should tell her what he was really thinking. They barely knew each other, and yet when they made love Greg felt as if she understood everything about him. Greg knew there had been other men before him— there had to be. But he never asked Gwen about them. He didn't want to torment himself with thoughts of old affairs that had nothing to do with the way Gwen felt about him.

Greg felt sure that she loved him, especially when they were making love. The interlude in the pine grove had just been the beginning. Now, whenever they were together, he ached to be holding her again, kissing her, adoring her. She gave herself to him so freely, so completely, as if whatever he wanted, she wanted just as passionately. Having Gwen had made it easier for him to accept the fact that Chris could never be his. And it made him yearn to possess her as totally, as surely, as Snapper possessed his wife.

"Come on, Greg," she coaxed again. "Tell me what you're thinking about—or is it a deep, dark secret? You haven't said a word since we came in here. Is something the matter?"

"Of course not." He squeezed her hand reassuringly. "I was just thinking about us."

"What about us?" she persisted, a flicker of fear coming into her eyes. Greg was the best thing that had ever happened to her; more than anything in the world, she was afraid of losing him.

"Actually, I've thought of the perfect solution to your landlord trouble."

"Terrific!" she beamed, relieved by his answer. "What is it?"

"I don't know if you're going to go for it, Gwen," he hedged, suddenly feeling as shy as a schoolboy. "It's not strictly a legal solution."

"I'm not sure I know what you're getting at," she admitted, a puzzled frown knitting her forehead.

Greg pulled her close and began to kiss the lines away, oblivious to the curious glances of the other customers. He wanted to go on kissing her—all over. Although she wasn't at all overweight, Gwen possessed a full, woman's body that could be both comforting and exciting, depending on his need. Just thinking about it made him stir with desire.

"I wish we could get out of here and talk someplace where we were alone." he murmured hungrily.

"Maybe tonight," she said daringly. Even though she knew she was playing with fire, she didn't want to disappoint him. "But it will have to be very late—four or five a.m.

She laughed, happy that he wanted her so much. Greg wasn't like the others. She was sure of it. He wanted her—not just what he could get from her. "But you can't keep me in suspense until then. What's your answer to my landlord's harassment?"

"It's simply, really—so simple I can't imagine why I didn't think of it the moment I saw you. You can marry me, Gwen. Then you won't need your apartment anymore."

"Marry you?" Gwen echoed. At his words her eyes had widened like circles and her face had turned so white that he was afraid she was going to faint.

"What's the matter?" Greg asked tensely. "I know it's sudden and all, but I didn't think it was such a terrible idea that you'd take offense or anything."

"Offense?" she repeated stupidly, shaking her head in disbelief. "Just because I'm not as good as you—that doesn't give you any right to play games with me."

"Is that what you think I'm doing—playing games with you?" Greg demanded, as incredulous now as she was. "I just proposed to you, Gwen." He found himself shouting in exasperation so loudly that customers at the neighboring tables turned to listen. "I asked you to marry me. To be my wife."

"You're going to marry me so that I won't get kicked out of my apartment. What kind of proposal is that?" she challenged, as angry now as he was. Her eyes blazed as brightly as her hair as she faced him defiantly.

Although he'd never asked her to, Gwen had taken to dressing more conservatively for him, and to wearing only the lightest make-up. Looking at her now, Greg thought that her outrage made her more beautiful than ever.

"Is that what you really believe?" he asked, more gently than before. "I asked you to marry me because I want to be with you all the time...not for a few hurried hours here and there. I know it's kind of sudden; we've only known each other for a few weeks. And I guess I blew it—I mean the way I brought up the subject and all. I'll try again if it will make you feel better," he offered hopefully.

"O.K.," she said, the mistrust still clear in her voice.

"Gwen Sherman," Greg began seriously, taking her hand in both of his. "Will you do me the honor of becoming my wife? I can't offer you much on the salary of a legal aid lawyer, but at least we'll be together all the time...and that's what I want more than anything."

Greg waited expectantly for the answer he hoped she'd give. But Gwen was waiting too, with just as much anticipation. "Didn't you forget to mention a very important thing?" she asked finally, the confident pose that she usually presented completely gone.

Greg tried to think, but he was as nervous as she was now, sure that she was going to reject him—just as Chris had. His heart, so freshly healed, began to lock shut again in anticipation of her answer. "Forget it, Gwen. I made a mistake," he was about to say, when a voice from a nearby table piped up, "You didn't tell her you loved her."

Both Gwen and Greg blushed together at the interruption. But even as he did, Greg whispered, "Do I have to tell you that, Gwen?"

She nodded her head vigorously. "Only if it's true," she answered, in a voice so small he barely recognized it.

"Well, it's true...if being in love with you means that I can't concentrate on anything except you. That I never want to stop touching you, holding you, kissing you, loving you. That even when I'm just thinking about you leaving, I begin to miss you. Is that good enough?"

Gwen nodded. The smile that had begun in her eyes as he spoke spread to her lips, lighting up her whole face.

"Then what's your answer?" Greg pressed, afraid to even hope.

"You can drop my case any time you like," she said, bursting into an exultant laugh. "The sooner my landlord evicts me, the happier I'll be."

For an instant he stared at her uncomprehendingly, then he threw his arms around her. "You mean yes? Your answer is yes?"

"I think you're nuts, Greg Foster, to want to marry a girl like me. But yes, yes, yes, yes," Gwen cried, happier than she had ever imagined she could be.

In her heart Gwen knew that she should say no to Greg. If he suspected what she really was, what she had been ever since she moved to Genoa City, he would never want her to be his wife. Marriage to Greg was a dream—and in the kind of life she lived, she'd learned that dreams never come true. But his proposal was so unexpected that for once she allowed herself to be carried away, forgetting the hard lessons she had learned. Somehow there must be a way, she told herself, and she would find it. Greg never had to know what she really was. Once they were married, she'd put the other life she had kept secret from him behind her forever and be the wife that he wanted. Until then...Gwen didn't want to think about that now. This was the happiest moment of her life, and she wouldn't let anyone spoil it—not even Duke Stevens. A shudder of fear swept over her at the thought of him, but Greg didn't notice. He was blind to everything except the sparkling, star-filled eyes of the girl he wanted to marry.

"I'm not nuts," he laughed, his lips reaching up to seal her promise with a kiss. "But I am crazy about you, Gwen Sherman," he murmured as his mouth closed over hers, blocking out every thought, every consideration, every secret, except the urgent song of their hearts beating in unison. Her lips were moist and as hungry as his own, and their kiss lingered and deepened. For that moment, the earth seemed to stop spinning. Time stood still; there existed only the two of them eternally united by a kiss that seemed to have no beginning and no end. Gradually, though, together they became aware of a sound that was intensifying and surrounding them. Reluctantly drawing apart, they realized with a flush of embarrassment that the other customers had broken into spontaneous applause.

"Drinks on the house," the bartender called, raising a glass in the direction of the blushing couple. "That was the best show I've seen in years."

With one arm hugging Gwen protectively, Greg waved his thanks to the spectators. "I couldn't have done it without you," he called jokingly.

Gwen beamed proudly at him, pinching herself to see if it were really happening to her. In her wildest dreams she had never imagined a man like Greg Foster proposing to her. He was handsome, honest, strong, gentle, kind, loving—everything she could ask for in a man, and a lawyer besides. He deserved to know the truth about the woman he was going to marry, Gwen told herself. Yet she knew she could never tell him. How could she expect him to understand what she had done...what she was still doing... what she would be forced to do this very night when she left him?

Jill Foster laid down her pen and wiped away the line of perspiration that had formed on her forehead. From the stack of mail still left in front of her, it seemed as if Kay Chancellor had neglected her correspondence for months. This is what it means to be rich, Jill thought, stretching wearily. You get requests for donations and joining committees from every charitable organization in the country. It seemed as if there were a society for every conceivable disease, cause, school and church—and every one of them had Mrs. Phillip Chancellor on its mailing list.

In the weeks that she had been employed in the Chancellors' house, Jill had scarcely made a dent in the mail. It seemed as if the more she answered, the more Kay Chancellor received.

But she had discovered the truth behind Phillip Chancellor's initial warning. The Chancellors' luxurious life was like a badly-constructed building—perfect on the outside but rotten within. A dream that turned out to be a nightmare—and all because Kay Chancellor could not control her lethal thirst. Jill had soon lost count of the number of liquor bottles she had discovered, hidden in the most unlikely places, and then poured down the toilet. Still, Kay always had one more that Jill had missed. And when she was done drinking, there was no predicting what she might say or do, or what demands she might make—especially on her employees. Her son, Brock, had left home, no doubt driven away by his mother's unbearable demands, Jill thought. Her husband refused to have anything more to do with her until she admitted her problem and accepted the help she so desperately needed. As a result there was nothing standing between Kay and her own total destruction—except Jill.

"Take care of Kay for me," Phillip Chancellor had said to her, and Jill had taken his words to heart. Now, putting away the stack of unanswered letters for another day, Jill went in search of her employer. No matter how busy she was, Jill made a point of interrupting her work every hour to check on Kay. It was almost like babysitting for an irresponsible child, Jill reminded herself, because once she began drinking Kay Chancellor had little control over her own actions. If she were going out for the afternoon, Jill made sure the chauffeur took her where she was going and waited to bring her

back. If she stayed home, Jill tried to keep an
eagle eye on her. Today, though, she had allowed
the time to slip away from her.

Running up the stairs, Jill checked Kay's room
and found it empty. There was no one in the
solarium, no one in the swimming pool, no one in
the den—the three places Kay was most likely to
be. Beginning her search again, Jill started
downstairs and looked in every room. Then she
went over the second floor just as thoroughly,
but Kay Chancellor was no place to be found.
Blaming herself for not having checked sooner,
Jill went outside. It wouldn't be long before
Phillip Chancellor would be home, and she didn't
want him to find his wife in a hopelessly drunken
state.

Spending each day in the Chancellors' home,
Jill had begun to fantasize that it was her own.
She'd never imagined that anyone lived that way
outside the movies, with a full household staff
just waiting to satisfy one's every whim. Each
room was lovelier than the next; each meal was
served on sterling silver platters; each trip, no
matter how short, was made in a chauffeured
car—if not a limousine, then at least a Mercedes.
One step outside the solarium and you could dive
into a heated swimming pool. A leisurely walk
through manicured gardens and you arrived at
the stables, where a half-dozen sleek Arabians
were waiting to be saddled.

Jill rushed past the pool and through the
garden paths, looking anxiously for some sign of
Kay. Once she was totally and completely
smashed, there was no predicting what she
might do. One afternoon Jill had found her naked

on an upstairs balcony. Another time she located her in the garage, trying to drive off in her husband's favorite car. Although she was fond of her employer, who in her lucid moments was a kind if imperious woman, Jill couldn't understand what made Kay drink. She had everything the world could offer, including a tender, thoughtful husband—how then could she be so unhappy, so dissatisfied, that she was compelled to destroy herself with alcohol, Jill wondered as she rushed on. If she were in Kay Chancellor's shoes, Jill was sure that she would be the happiest woman in the world.

Even though she knew it was wrong, Jill couldn't keep herself from imagining what it would be like to have nothing to do all day except enjoy herself, and nothing to do all evening except make herself beautiful for her husband— Phillip Chancellor. All her dreams included him. To Jill he seemed as perfect as his home. He was quiet and considerate, yet at the same time exciting, controlling a wealthy empire with ease. Now he was on his way home. How could she face him and admit that his wife was nowhere to be found? He had trusted her to control Kay—a difficult position for someone so young, but one that Jill took very seriously. And she didn't want to fail him.

The low, red-roofed stables spread out just ahead of her as Jill hurried on. They were the last place left where she could think to look for Kay, and she didn't really expect to find her employer there. The stables were Phillip Chancellor's domain. Kay had little or no interest in the horses, and there was nothing else there really, except...

Jill stopped suddenly. She uttered out loud a low exclamation of disbelief as the gossip she'd overheard in the beauty salon came rushing back to her. "No! She wouldn't!" Jill repeated to herself. Although she was afraid of what she might discover and didn't want to go any farther, Jill forced herself to walk deliberately toward the stables.

Swallowing hard, she pushed open the heavy door a crack and slid inside. The heady odor of hay and manure assailed her immediately, and she stepped gingerly toward the stalls. A horse whinnied as if in greeting, startling her; otherwise, the place seemed empty. As her eyes adjusted to the dimmer light Jill looked around, her fearful anticipation changing to relief. There was no sign of Kay Chancellor. If the stableboy were around, Jill would ask him if he'd seen Mrs. Chancellor. Otherwise, she'd go back to the house and begin her search there again.

Jill had seen the stableboy only once—on her first day at the Chancellors' when she'd wandered through the grounds waiting for Mrs. Chancellor to wake up. She remembered him unpleasantly as a muscular boy, not much older than she, with a shock of dirty-blond hair and a sullen expression. He'd made a lewd remark to her as she approached. So, instead of inspecting the stables as Phillip Chancellor had suggested she should do, Jill had turned around and gone back to the pool, wishing she'd brought her bathing suit with her. At the time it had never occurred to her that the Chancellors kept a full supply of bathing suits for men and women in every size in the adjoining cabanas.

Now she braced herself, prepared to endure his grossness if he could help her find Kay. Walking past the stalls, hugging the outer wall of the stable for fear that one of the horses might kick out at her, Jill came to a ladder that led up to a hayloft. Beyond it stretched a row of empty stalls. Deciding that it was pointless to look any further, she started to turn back, when an unexpected noise stopped her.

At first Jill thought it was the low moan of an animal in distress. Then, listening more closely, she realized it was a human voice, and that it was coming from the empty stalls beyond. She hesitated at first. Then, summoning her courage, she crept stealthily toward the sound. Mrs. Chancellor might be hurt, she told herself, or she might have passed out. But deep inside Jill was afraid that the reality was even worse.

As she edged closer to the empty stalls, the sound grew louder, more intense. She recognized the moaning voice and the shriek of pain that followed. It was deep and husky, yet distinctly female—Kay Chancellor. Jill began to rush toward her. But a second, cruel male voice stopped her.

"You wanted me to hurt you, didn't you? You're always asking me to punish you. Well, this time I'm giving you as good as your word!" A harsh laugh froze Jill where she stood, and a wave of nausea swept over her. More than anything Jill wanted to rush out into the fresh, clear sunshine and not stop until she had put miles and miles between herself and the dark, desperate problems that haunted the Chancellor home. But a sharp, cracking sound stopped her.

With horror she saw the tongue of a black horsewhip snap across the top of the empty stall. Then Kay Chancellor's slurred yet still commanding voice shouted; "Bastard. Who do you think you are? I can replace you tomorrow with a dozen others better than you."

"You wouldn't like me to tell your husband about your afternoon visits, would you?" The answering voice was wheedling now, but still filled with arrogance. "This is what you want. You know it is." The whip snapped again, cutting the air sharply.

Fighting back the urge to retch convulsively, Jill forced herself to go toward the sickening sounds. "Mrs. Chancellor," she called into the dusky void, not wanting to actually see the picture that was being enacted just a few steps away. "It's me...Jill."

The silence that greeted her words was so pervasive that Jill thought for a moment they hadn't heard her. Then a threatening voice snarled back at her. "Get out of here and mind your damn business. There's no Mrs. Chancellor here."

Fear and revulsion gripped Jill, making her breath come in short, painful gasps. "Mrs. Chancellor," she called again, her voice quavering. "I know you're in here. And I'm coming after you," she added, summoning a courage she wasn't sure she possessed.

Before she could take a step closer, the answer to her second cry loomed up in front of her, his sullen face creased in a sneer of angry contempt. The stableboy came toward her, his thick work boots clomping across the hard cement floor.

Clumps of blond hair curled out of his soiled undershirt. Although Jill tried not to look, Jill couldn't help noticing that he hadn't bothered to close his jeans. Furled menacingly in his dirty hands was the leather horsewhip.

Instinctively, Jill backed away from him.

"What do you want, Miss Busybody?" he demanded, closing the distance between them with sure, dangerous strides, at the same time hitting the whip handle against his open palm as if he were deciding whether or not to use it on her.

"Mrs. Chancellor?" Although Jill tried to make her voice sound as defiant as his, it trembled with fear.

"I told you, she's not here. Now get out if you know what's good for you...and keep your mouth shut." He brandished the whip just inches from her pale face.

But Jill stood her ground. "You're lying," she accused him. "I know Mrs. Chancellor is here. I heard her screaming...and I heard you threatening her."

"You're hearing things, girlie...understand?" The stableboy was so close to Jill now that she could see the light stubble on his cheeks and smell the mixture of sweat and sex on his body.

"I'm not leaving here until Mrs. Chancellor goes with me," she insisted, with more conviction than she felt.

"I get it." His lips pulled back across his small teeth. "You want to come in and join us, don't you? Well, come on then, why didn't you say so?" His hand closed around her arm and he yanked her forward. "Two are better than one, that's what I always say." He laughed harshly, tightening his grip on her.

Jill tried to scream and pull free of him. But when she opened her mouth, no sound emerged. Silently she struggled against his superior strength, but she was no match for him. And she realized with a renewed surge of terror that he could do anything he wanted to her. She was powerless against him.

"Leave her alone!" Suddenly the tall, imposing figure of Kay Chancellor lurched from the empty stall. "This moment! Do you hear me?" Although her clothing was disheveled and wisps of hay clung to her hair, her voice still snapped as sharply as the whip.

"I just thought we could have some fun...the three of us." The stableboy's voice turned to a whine, but he let go of Jill's arm.

She staggered back from him, her enormous, dark eyes fixed on Kay Chancellor. "I've been looking for you everywhere," Jill stammered shakily.

"Next time, don't bother," Kay warned darkly. "I didn't hire you to be my keeper."

"But Mr. Chancellor called. He's on his way home. In fact, he's probably here by now."

A loud, scornful laugh greeted Jill's words. "And you thought you were protecting me from my husband's wrath?" Kay laughed again, a sound more bitter than any Jill had ever heard. "Don't you understand yet, Jill dear?" She staggered forward and draped an arm across the girl's shoulders. "Phillip Chancellor isn't any kind of a husband to me. It's his way of punishing me for being a naughty girl. So I come down here to his favorite place to punish him back. But the funny thing is, Phillip doesn't give a damn what I do. I could have a dozen stableboys, and he wouldn't pay the slightest attention. A marriage made in heaven!"

She laughed again and swayed toward the stable door, pulling Jill with her. "Come on, Jill," she slurred. "We'd better get back...I need another drink. And so do you."

Chapter Six

Bitter Losses

Leslie stared out of the high curtained window at the gray, autumnal day. A cold drizzle was falling, marking the window with tiny drops as fine as grains of sand. Below, Fifth Avenue was lined with taxis, so that it resembled a long, narrow ribbon. Central Park stretched across the street as far as she could see. The brilliant hues of fall had faded, leaving only lusterless leaves clinging to the dark branches.

Leslie knew she should be excited. It was her first trip to New York, and the very next night she was scheduled to perform on the recital stage at Carnegie Hall—an opportunity any young pianist would seize gratefully. Instead, she felt tired and listless. Ever since her opening night concert in Detroit, she'd grown increasingly depressed—and it showed in her music. After that glorious debut when she was heralded as a major new talent, her performances had been competent but uninspired. Her technique was flawless, but as a critic in Boston wrote, "Miss Brooks played as if she had forgotten her heart in her hotel room."

Leslie knew she wasn't playing well, yet she seemed powerless to do anything about it. The concert schedule was proving to be a grueling one. When she finished a performance, she would go back to her hotel room and sink into bed, often skipping supper entirely. But no matter how many hours she slept, she'd wake up the next day feeling exhausted. Her weight dropped precariously, and she sank deeper and deeper into a depression. By the time she'd reached New York, Leslie had withdrawn completely into her private shell. Except for the recitals, she avoided all human contact. She even began to instruct the hotel operators to hold any calls for her so that she wouldn't have to put up an enthusiastic front for her parents when they made their daily phone call to her. When her tour manager would question her unusual behavior, Leslie would insist that she was just tired and retreat immediately to her room to rest. Until New York, he'd dismissed her poor performances and reclusive ways as artistic temperament. But with the important Carnegie Hall concert a mere twenty-four hours away and Leslie acting more and more despondent, he placed an urgent person-to-person call to Stuart Brooks in Genoa City.

Stuart and Jennifer Brooks were disappointed that they hadn't been able to attend as many of Leslie's concerts as they'd hoped to. But they spoke to her regularly and followed her progress carefully. Secretly, Stuart had been planning to make it up to his daughter for missing so many performances by flying into New York for her grand finale, and then staying on for a wonderful, much-needed weeklong vacation before bringing her home to Genoa City. But her manager's unexpected call accelerated his plans. Stuart and Jennifer Brooks caught the next available flight to Kennedy International Airport. If Leslie was in trouble, they wanted to be with her.

Ignorant of her manager's worried move, Leslie continued to stare fixedly out of her hotel room window as if her sunken, vacant eyes were glued to the wet pane. Although the room was a spacious double with an awesome view of New York and was decorated in a cool ice-blue with elegant French provincial furnishings and tasteful botanical floral prints on the walls, Leslie felt as if she were suffocating. She knew she should lie down and rest for the next night, but every time she stretched out on one of the beds, the walls seemed to close in on her. She felt restless and strange, as if she were confined in a small box and couldn't escape. Her family, her home, even Brad seemed so far away—as if they belonged to another person, another lifetime. Her pain was so deep that she had forced everything and everyone out of her mind, until now she felt only emptiness and intense despair. She had to get away—away from the bland hotel room, away from herself.

Impulsively, Leslie rushed out into the corridor and into the waiting elevator. In spite of the damp, chilly weather, she didn't take a coat. Outside the hotel, she darted across Fifth Avenue, mindless of the oncoming traffic. The alarmed doorman shouted at her and raced to the curb with an umbrella to shelter her. But it was too late. Leslie was halfway across the street, oblivious to the deafening screech of brakes and the angry screams of the drivers who were forced to stop short to avoid hitting her.

"You'll catch your death," the doorman shouted after her.

Leslie never heard him. She had reached the relative safety of the opposite sidewalk and was disappearing into Central Park. A biting wind whipped down from the reservoir through the old zoo's picturesque, wrought iron Victorian cages, furling discarded candy wrappers and papers around her ankles. Leslie didn't stop to admire the monkeys, acknowledge the teasing chatter of the gorilla or shrink from the hungry growl of the polar bear. Head down, eyes fixed on the wet leaves covering the path at her feet, she walked aimlessly on and on.

The drizzle soaked through the thin blouse and skirt she was wearing and dampened her long, thick hair, making it curl around her face in tiny tendrils. Although she shivered as each fresh blast of wind buffeted her, she seemed unconscious of the rain or the cold, unaware either of the gathering darkness or the path down which her steps were leading her. Wandering aimlessly, she passed the handsome old carousel, the music now quieted, horses motionless for the night; she crisscrossed the bridle path, empty of the chic riders formally dressed in jodphurs and hard velvet hats, then circled the ghostly bandshell, silhouetted silver-gray in the fading light. Strangely, Leslie felt freer than she had in weeks, as if she'd been trying and trying and had finally succeeded in escaping. But from what? From whom? Her forehead knitted intensely as she tried to think. But no memories would come...

Miles away, high above the blanket of clouds that covered this island of Manhattan, the jet carrying Jennifer and Stuart Brooks soared eastward. Although her seatbelt was still fastened, Jennifer clung to her husband's arm. She had no fear of flying. In fact, she was so preoccupied that she scarcely realized there was a bank of clouds beneath her. All of her intense fear was for Leslie. The concern that she had felt leaving her daughter after the first concert in Detroit returned more strongly than ever before. It had been a week since they'd even spoken to Leslie. She was out whenever they called, and Leslie never found time to return their calls. Imagining that her daughter was being wined and dined and celebrated for the exceptional talent that she was, Jennifer had been pleased...and relieved. If she didn't speak to Leslie, she wouldn't have to break Laurie's news to her. Jennifer was still stunned by the unexpected turn her daughters' lives had taken.

Leslie was supposed to marry Brad. And now the wedding was going on as previously planned—only this time the bride was going to be Laurie. It had all been so sudden. One day Jennifer was leaving Leslie in Detroit, heartsick because Brad hadn't shown up at her concert; the next she was returning home to be met by a beaming Laurie and her unexpected bombshell. Maybe, thought Jennifer, she was hopelessly old-fashioned, but it smacked too much of musical chairs—or worse, musical beds—for her taste. Still, she was reluctant to interfere. Was Leslie wrong for Brad...and Laurie right? Had he used Leslie heartlessly; was he perhaps now doing the very same thing to her sister? Or had Brad realized the mistake he was making and stepped aside to spare Leslie the pain of an unhappy marriage only to find later, in Laurie, what he had been searching for?

Jennifer rubbed her forehead to ease the tension headache that was gathering strength like a storm, and looked anxiously at her husband. Stuart Brooks had studiously avoided discussing the subject of Laurie's sudden engagement to Brad Elliot. And Jennifer had decided to wait until he was ready. Now, though, winging nearer and nearer to Leslie, she couldn't help pressing the issue.

"What do you think we should do, Stu?" she began nervously. "I mean about Laurie and Brad. Should we tell Leslie about it now or wait until we get her home?"

"I think that bit of news should come from Brad and Laurie—not from us," he answered thoughtfully. "I'm still trying to figure out how it happened. I know you have reservations about Brad Elliot, but I've worked with a lot of men, and there isn't one I have more respect for than Brad. He's just not the kind of guy to do anything underhanded. I've thought about having a talk with him, but what could I say? 'How dare you love two of my daughters? Don't you know that will destroy my family?' " Stuart Brooks shook his head in puzzlement. "I can understand having a good time when you're young, Jen. But try as I may, I can't understand loving two women. With me there was only you. I never had a doubt or a second thought."

Jennifer squeezed his hand, partly out of gratitude and partly out of guilt. She couldn't say the same to her husband. Even after so many years of marriage, she couldn't say that she had loved only him—without lying.

"And what about Laurie?" Stuart went on as if he were thinking aloud, going over the same questions he'd asked himself a million times. "Have you talked to her seriously? Doesn't she have any regard for her sister's feelings?"

"Sometimes I think we made a mistake giving Laurie permission to go to Paris. It changed her," Jennifer said, choosing her words carefully.

"She grew up over there."

"Yes. Too fast and in too many ways. Sometimes, trying to talk to her now, I think I don't know my own daughter any more. In a year away she became a stranger and..." Jennifer stopped herself, afraid of admitting something she would regret.

"And what, Jen?" Stuart pressed.

"Nothing...I don't know." Jennifer evaded his eyes. "I'm just worried about Leslie."

Her husband ignored her excuse. "You were going to say, 'a not altogether likeable stranger,' weren't you?"

When Jennifer nodded, he closed his eyes, as reluctant as she was to admit what he truly felt, yet knowing that he had to. "Sometimes, even watching Laurie in the office, I get the uncomfortable impression that she would do anything—anything at all—to get what she wanted."

"And you think that's how she got Brad?" Jennifer's voice was like a hushed whisper. She'd never expected to hear herself speaking so coldly about one of her own children.

"A man has to be responsible for his own actions—especially for whom he chooses to marry," Stuart answered, the firmness in his voice making it clear that the topic was closed to further discussion, at least for the time being.

Jennifer didn't press her husband, unwilling to have to admit any more of her deepest feelings. Laurie was her daughter as much as Leslie, and she didn't want to be forced to choose between them. "United we stand; divided we fall," she thought with a tremor of apprehension as the 707 jet began banking sharply.

The voice of the stewardess sounded over the intercom, reminding the passengers to fasten their seat belts and extinguish all cigarettes for the descent into Kennedy Airport. Looking out the window, Jennifer saw the lights from the airport glimmering below like so many fallen stars. In an hour they would see Leslie again. It seemed as if her tour had lasted forever, but now... With a rush of pleasure, Jennifer imagined Leslie's surprise to see them a day earlier than expected, never suspecting that her fragile, first-born daughter had passed beyond surprises or disappointments into a remote, unexplored realm they could not enter.

"Where are you going, Miss? Don't you know it's dangerous to walk through the park alone at night like this?" A blue patrol car pulled up beside Leslie, the revolving red light on its roof casting eerie shadows on the deserted road. Through the loudspeaker, the officer's voice echoed with sudden, unexpected loudness.

Leslie wasn't startled, though. Instead, she walked on as if she hadn't even noticed the intrusion. The patrol car inched along beside her. Still, she didn't look up.

"Get in. I'll take you wherever you're going," the inhuman voice called out again.

This time Leslie looked all around her like a person in a daze. For a moment she lifted up her face and let the cold, light drizzle fall over it. Caught in the arc of a streetlamp, like a doe in the headlight of a car, she appeared lost and helpless.

The officers pulled their car over against the curb and got out. Both rookies, they were convinced that if they didn't do something with the girl, they'd be filing a rape report—or worse—before their tour of duty was over that night.

"What's your name, Miss?" one of them asked.

The gentleness of his voice seemed to catch Leslie's attention and she looked at him with huge, empty eyes. "My name?" she repeated blankly.

"Do you live around here?" the other followed up.

"Live...?" her voice trailed off. "I'm not sure," she murmured in confusion. "I can't seem to remember...Where am I? In the country?"

"No, ma'am," the first officer responded quickly. "More like the jungle at this time of night. You're in Central Park in New York City. Are you feeling all right?" he added, eying her closely.

"I just can't remember." She ran her hand over her eyes as if she were trying to wipe away the cobwebs, then stared up at them, frightened eyes darting back and forth between the two men. "I think I went out for a walk...I had to get away...The walls were closing in on me...They were trapping me...I must have gotten lost..."

The desperate urgency in her voice sent a shiver of horror down the young officers' spines. The girl was beautiful, with her hair curling in ringlets around a face as fragile as a petal, long lashes shining in the misty rain blinking over eyes as wide as a lake—beautiful and insane. Something in her had to have snapped for her to be walking where she was, in this weather, wearing only a thin blouse and skirt. New York! —you never knew what you'd find on any night.

"Try to remember...at least who you are... your name and address...so we can take you home," one of them urged.

But Leslie could only stare at them and shake her head helplessly. A curtain had fallen across her memory, blocking out the heartache, the disappointment that had become too intense to bear any longer. She felt empty but no longer sad. Instead, a strange peacefulness had descended over her.

Looking at the two young men dressed identically in navy uniforms with gleaming brass buttons, she knew they would help her. They would take her home—wherever that was— show her the way, and then she would remember. She must have a name; everyone had a name. For the first time, she smiled shyly at them, feeling foolish for not being able to tell them whether

her name was Anne, or Margaret, or something exotic like Eugenia.

"Come on," one of the officers was saying, taking her arm. "We'll give you a ride."

"Where are you taking me?" she asked when she had settled back comfortably in the warm, dry car. "Home?"

"A home of a sort, I guess," the driver answered, the reluctance clear in his voice. "At least it's a place where you may be able to get some help. That's the best I can promise."

Leslie sank back against the seat and closed her eyes. She felt colder in the warm car than she had walking through the park, but the officers were so kind she didn't want to sound ungrateful by complaining.

"Car 974 heading southeast with a female passenger, picked up wandering in the park," the second officer spoke into a receiver. "Destination: Bellevue Hospital."

"Bellevue...beautiful vista," Leslie thought wearily as the car sped out of the park. What a lovely name to give her home, wherever it was.

Chapter Seven

Illicit Love

It was Indian summer in Genoa City. October had rushed in, bringing with it a burst of warm weather. The rising mercury made it seem as if the calendar were lying. The month should read August, not October, for it was more like beach than pumpkin weather. Summer clothes, already packed away for another year, were pulled out again. Birds which had already begun their winter migration stopped in mid-flight, no longer certain in which direction to fly. In gardens all over town, zinnias and dahlias enjoyed a second brilliant flowering, and the leaves held onto the trees, refusing to change colors.

Although the Chancellors' swimming pool was heated, the sun was strong enough to do the job unassisted. Jill floated on her back, carried through the turquoise water as much by her dreams as by the striped canvas raft on which she was lying. Kay had gone off to an engagement luncheon in honor of Laurie Brooks, telling Jill to take the afternoon off and enjoy herself. Since the sordid episode in the stables Jill had been watching her like a hawk, trying, at the same time, to reinterest Phillip Chancellor in his wife's condition. Her success was spotty. Although Kay continued to get drunk almost daily, her behavior was more discreet. But Phillip seemed to have closed his heart to her.

Even with the sun beaming directly down on her, Jill shivered at the thought of Phillip Chancellor. He was a quiet, soft-spoken man on the surface. But she remembered her mother's saying: "Still waters run deep." Although she knew she was behaving like a schoolgirl with a crush on a movie star, Jill couldn't keep him out of her dreams. In her starry eyes he seemed like the perfect man—glamorous, handsome, sophisticated and kind—except where his wife was concerned. Although he listened with discomforting intensity to every report Jill gave him, when she was finished he would always give the same reply: "Kay's problem is her own. You're very good to her, Jill, but in the end only she can help herself."

Thinking about it now, his answer sounded cold, even heartless. But when he gave it, his eyes holding her more inescapably than any man's arms ever had, Jill always felt an inexplicable rush of warmth. Phillip Chancellor! She paddled the water with her hands to move the raft faster and let herself dream. What would it be like to be married to a man like him? Although he was old enough to be her father, she was sure it would be pure heaven. Instinctively, she ran her hands down her body, every fluid line clearly delineated by the simple tank suit. Although all her high school friends were doing it, Jill had resisted the pressure to have sex just to be one of the crowd. She didn't want her first time to be in a souped-up car with some guy she didn't care a thing about, drinking a six-pack of beer and then climbing into the back seat. Still, she couldn't help wondering what it was like. What it would be like with a man like. . .

A light breeze had come up and the raft was drifting toward the deep end of the pool. As it knocked lightly against the side, a shadow fell across it. Shivering, Jill opened her eyes, expecting to see a cluster of clouds overhead. Instead, she found herself looking up at the man she had been fantasizing about. Phillip Chancellor had a huge green terry cloth bath sheet open for her, but it was the expression on his face that held Jill, causing the color to rise slowly to her cheeks. He was looking at her in a way he'd never looked before—a way that made her keenly aware of how revealing her suit clung to her body, how little there was protecting her from the burning embers of his eyes.

"Come out now, Jill," he commanded in a low, almost gruff voice, "before you catch pneumonia. It may feel like August but it's still October, you know."

"Mrs. Chancellor told me to enjoy myself," she said defensively as she pulled herself over the edge of the pool. His expression and voice were so strained that she was afraid he might be angry because he had caught her loafing.

"Where is my wife now?"

"She went to an engagement party. . .for Laurie Brooks."

"You should have gone with her," he murmured as much to himself as to her, "instead of..." His voice trailed off as he wrapped the towel around her, folding her in it and gently pulling it closer to him. With the corner of the towel he reached up and dried her face with a tenderness so unexpected that she felt strange tingling sensations like tiny darts of fire shooting through her body.

"You're trembling," he said, wrapping her tighter. "You've probably caught cold already."

"It's not the cold," she admitted, turning away from him quickly, too inexperienced to know how to handle the unfamiliar feelings his closeness was stirring inside her. "I'd better go and change now."

Without waiting for him to reply, Jill skirted the edge of the pool, keenly aware of the swift, padding sound of her own feet as she retreated to the safety of the cabana. Inside she stopped short, still hugging the bath sheet around her shivering shoulders as waves of relief and disappointment washed over her. Why had she run away from Phillip Chancellor? Was she excited... afraid? The emotions colliding inside her were creating new, powerful sensations she didn't fully understand.

Jill wasn't sure how long she stood in the middle of the cabana, her body trembling uncontrollably. But when she finally turned around to close the door, he was standing there, watching her, his eyes soft yet at the same time hungry. Without a word he stepped in, shutting the door behind him.

"You're home early, Mr. Chancellor," she said,

feeling how foolish the words sounded even as she spoke them.

"Haven't you noticed, Jill? I've been coming home early every day since you came to work here. I find myself distracted from everything else because I'm thinking of you. You must have felt it, too. I know you have," he murmured, coming toward her.

Jill knew she should do something, but she couldn't make her body move away from him. It was as if it possessed a will of its own.

"Mr. Chancellor!" she whispered, her heart pounding.

"Phillip," he corrected her, tilting up her chin so that his lips could cover hers. The softness and warmth of them surprised her, and she felt her whole being awaken to sensations she'd never even imagined.

Jill tried to hold back. But her body rebelled, refusing to struggle, refusing to deny him. As in a dream, her lips answered him, opening just a crack at first, then wider. With a deep sensual moan of pleasure her body thrust toward his, needing to feel more than his lips on her. The towel dropped unnoticed from her shoulders as her arms circled his neck, sure that was where they belonged.

When their kiss finally ended, Jill's body was trembling more violently than before, aroused with a fire that seemed to sear every nerve ending.

"Never run away from me again, Jill," Phil whispered. "Not now. I couldn't bear it." As he spoke, he reached up and slipped her bathing suit straps over her shoulders. As she moved toward him, his arms moved to meet her, to pull her vibrant pulsating body close to his.

Jill knew she should stop him before it was too late. But she wanted him to go on forever. She wanted Phillip to kiss her, to hold her and fondle her, to never stop. "Phil, Phil," she murmured again and again, kissing his dark hair as he bent over her. But when he moved even closer, an alarm sounded with her.

"No, Phil, we can't," she insisted, stopping his hands with her own.

"Please, Jill," he begged. Nonetheless, he released her, wanting her to give herself freely to him because she wanted and needed him.

Feeling bereft without his touch, Jill hugged herself, suddenly embarrassed. "What about Kay? She's your wife."

He pulled her hands away from her body and pressed one against each of her cheeks. "I loved Kay once, very much. She was beautiful and fearless and honest. But that died a long time ago. There was nothing left between us except bitterness. Then you came into this house—like a breath of fresh air in this fetid, heartless place. Kissing you now, I felt as if I had died and come back to life. You brought me back, Jill. Don't deny me now."

She reached up and touched his pleading eyes, wanting to say 'yes' to him, yet knowing she couldn't. She shouldn't. For all her faults, Kay Chancellor had always treated Jill well. She couldn't sneak behind her back and steal her husband. "Kay is sick. She needs our help," Jill insisted.

"I need you, too," he reminded her, knowing

even as he spoke that she was right.

Jill shook her head. "We can never be free to love each other until Kay is cured. Once she's strong enough to stand on her own feet again, then. . ."

"That could take forever," he replied sadly. Stooping down, he picked up the towel and wrapped it around her shoulders again, covering her. "I've taken her to doctors, psychiatrists, psychologists, ministers, clinics. It's no use."

"We'll find a way. We *have* to," she insisted, too young to be able to accept defeat.

For a moment longer, Phillip held the ends of the towel, searching her face for the answer his heart yearned to hear. "Is there someone else, Jill? Because if there is, I want you to tell me now."

She smiled up at him, the fullness of her heart reflected in her face. "There never was—and there never can be, now that you have kissed me."

Wrapping his arms around her, he held her close, unwilling to ever let her go.

Greg Foster tapped on his water glass with the blade of his knife to get his family's attention. It was a rare Sunday dinner. All the Fosters were home, even Snapper and his wife, and Liz Foster had splurged for the occasion, roasting a chicken and making all the fixings that went with it— even cranberry sauce.

"I have an important announcement to make," Greg said, looking around the table from one to the other.

"Well, don't keep us in suspense," Jill rejoined,

"What is it?"

The hint of a blush tinged Greg's cheeks and he cleared his throat ceremoniously. "Believe it or not, I'm finally taking the big step. I'm getting married!"

"That's wonderful, Greg," Chris beamed across the table at him, her enormous eyes sparkling like sapphires. "Who's the lucky girl?"

"Actually, she's a client of mine. She came to me with a legal problem. One thing sort of led to another, and the next thing I knew I heard myself proposing to her. I know you're going to like her, Mom," he added, turning to his mother. "Everyone will. She's one swell lady—just a farm girl really, from Michigan. Her name is Gwen Sherman."

The three women started talking at once, firing excited questions at Greg in rapid succession. "What's she like? How old is she? What does she do? When's the wedding?"

"Hold it! Hold it!" Greg cried, laughing and holding up his hands as if to ward off an attack. "One at a time, ladies, please. Mom first."

But instead of asking Greg about his bride-to-be, Mrs. Foster turned to her older son. Since the night she found Snapper and Greg fighting in her kitchen, she had watched her two sons warily, afraid that another fight might erupt. "You're unusually quiet, Snapper," she said. "Aren't you going to congratulate your brother?"

Snapper was holding his glass between his hands as if he might crush it at any moment. Instead of answering his mother, he turned to Greg slowly. "What did you say her name was?"

"Gwen Sherman," Greg repeated, too excited

to notice his brother's taut expression. "And I'd hate to have to choose who was prettier—Gwen or Chris. Or Mom or Jill," he added, flashing them both an enormous grin. "Why don't you tell us what she looks like?" Snapper pressed.

"She's tall," Greg began, "and...I don't know how to describe a girl," he laughed self-consciously. "She's got long red hair. I guess that's the first thing anybody would notice."

Snapper's fingers tightened around his glass with shattering impact. Shards of broken glass flew across the table in every direction and scattered on the floor. Chris stifled a cry of horror as a small geyser of blood sprang up from his palm.

"It's nothing...just a scratch," he insisted, wrapping his napkin around it and pushing back his chair. "Greg will doctor me up, lawyer that he is."

"Sure, Snapper" Greg jumped up to help his brother.

"Come on," Snapper said tensely while the others scrambled to clean up the mess he had made. "Let's get out of here. I have to talk to you."

"But your hand," Greg protested.

"Forget it. That was just an excuse to get you alone."

"What's the matter, Snapper?" Greg looked worriedly from his brother's tense face to the circle of blood widening on his napkin.

"Want to take a ride?" he replied non-committally, leading the way out to the front steps.

"Now?" Greg sounded incredulous. "Mom

baked a cake for dessert especially because you and Chris were coming."

"The cake can wait," Snapper muttered, easing himself down on the top step.

"I don't understand what happened all of a sudden," Greg sat down beside him. "You acted so strange in there."

"I just want you to tell me something, Greg, that's all," Snapper said, facing his brother squarely. "How much do you know about this Gwen Sherman?"

"What do you mean?" Greg demanded, instantly ready to defend Gwen against whatever objections he sensed Snapper was about to make. "I know she's a terrific lady...and she loves me. What else matters?"

"I mean, what does she do for a living? That kind of thing." Snapper's voice was tense. He hoped he was wrong. He hoped, for his brother's sake, that there was another girl named Sherman with red hair in Genoa City. Ever since their fistfight over Chris there had been a certain distance, a distinct coolness between the Foster brothers. Although he knew he was at least partially responsible for it, Snapper had been wishing he could find a way to get close to Greg again. Instead, he was afraid he was going to push his brother further away. If Gwen was the girl he thought she was, then what Snapper was about to reveal could only increase Greg's bitterness.

"She does clerical work," Greg answered. "I don't see what difference that makes, though. She's not a doctor, a lawyer, or an Indian chief— how many girls are?"

"Hold on, brother," Snapper put a calming hand on Greg's arm. "I don't have anything against the lady. I just want to be sure you know what you're getting into."

"You don't always have to play the big brother with me. I'm not twelve years old anymore," Greg bristled.

"O.K. Sometimes, I admit, I may lay it on too thick, but just bear with me this time. Please, Greg."

Snapper's concern sounded so genuine that Greg was touched. "O.K. I'm sorry," he said sheepishly. "What else do you want to know?"

"Well, clerical work is a little broad, don't you think? I mean, where's her office, who does she work for, where does she live?"

"Actually," Greg admitted, "I don't really know who her employer is. I guess the subject never came up. The whole thing has been so fast, so intense, I haven't had time to think about details like that. I've only known Gwen a couple of months. The truth is, I didn't even realize I was going to propose to her until I heard myself saying the words."

"And now that you have?"

"I'm happier than I ever imagined I could be...I mean, with anyone except Chris."

Greg and Snapper had never talked about Chris since the night of their fight. In fact, they'd barely spoken at all. But now that Snapper seemed to be so genuinely concerned about his future, Greg decided to be completely honest, no matter how painful it was or how hard on his pride.

Snapper squeezed his brother's shoulder,

understanding how much it had cost Greg to make that admission, and wondering if he would have been so frank had their places been reversed. "Come on, Greg, you must know something else about the girl you're going to marry?" he pressed.

"Honest, I don't. She came to me because her landlord's threatening eviction, because she's been late with her rent a couple of times. It must be tough to try and make it all alone on a clerk-typist's salary—even with overtime. Gwen works so hard, sometimes I wonder why she doesn't simply keel over from exhaustion. Five and six nights a week, even Saturdays and Sundays, she puts in overtime. I have to marry her," he laughed. "It's the only way I'm going to get to see her for more than an hour or two in the afternoon."

In spite of Greg's light, joking tone, Snapper's face had darkened ominously. "Let me get this straight, Greg," he began, running both hands through his thick, dark hair nervously. "You and Gwen never go out at night?"

"We can't," Greg insisted, his defensiveness returning as he sensed Snapper's unease. "I told you Gwen puts in an awful lot of overtime."

"Are you sure that's what she's doing every night—weekends too?" Snapper's question sounded sharper than he intended, firing his brother's resentment again.

"Just what are you getting at?" he asked angrily, his defenses aroused.

"Does Gwen have a nickname?" Snapper asked, instead of answering his question.

"Not that I know of," Greg responded

grudgingly. The more questions Snapper asked, the more he realized he didn't know very much about Gwen after all.

"You ever hear anybody call her 'Scarlet Sherman'?"

Greg hesitated. "I guess somebody did, once," he admitted. "We passed some guy on the street and he called out a macho remark. I guess he was an old boyfriend, because Gwen got really uptight when I asked her about it and told me never to call her 'Scarlet'."

"What did the guy say?" Snapper buried his face in his hands and spoke through them so that his voice sounded muffled and distant.

"You know the usual," Greg tried to remember. "Save some for me, Scarlet! Something like that."

"*Christ,*" Snapper muttered, grinding his knuckles into his eyes.

"What's the matter? What are you getting at anyway, Snapper?" Greg demanded, his brother's tension beginning to rub off on him. "Do you know something about Gwen I don't?"

Snapper's head nodded mutely, and he looked at his brother with dark, burning eyes. "I wish to God I didn't, Greg," he said bleakly. "If you hadn't been away from Genoa City so long, you'd probably know about her yourself. There aren't many men in town who don't know Scarlet Sherman—at least by reputation."

"What are you getting at, Snapper?" Greg's voice was filled with anger—and fear.

"Gwen's a hooker, Greg," Snapper said flatly. "She works downtown in the better areas. She used to hang out on the corner near Frenchy's Restaurant. That's where I'd see her. Since

Frenchy's closed, she must have found a new corner," he rushed on, spilling everything out in one breath, and looking straight ahead so that he wouldn't have to see his brother's face. "I don't know. You'll have to ask her that yourself. But obviously she's still in action if she's working six nights out of seven. She's not putting in overtime, Greg," he said disgustedly, "she's available for any man with a twenty-dollar bill to spare. Lucking on to you—an Ivy League lawyer with stars in his eyes—must be like stumbling onto a pot of gold for somebody like Scarlet Sherman. That's how she's known downtown—Scarlet. The name kind of goes with the territory, if you know what I mean."

"Stop it!" Greg ground out the two short words sharply. "I'm not going to listen to another word. I don't believe it. It can't be Gwen. It's got to be somebody else."

But even as he shouted out his bitter denials, Greg's mind was racing. Every terrible lie Snapper had told him rang with the death knell of truth. It all fit so neatly. The way Gwen was dressed the first time she went to his office: a tight leather mini skirt, spiked heels, a sweater two sizes too small, thick make-up. The late night hours she worked. Even the way she made love. From the very first time in the pine grove she seemed to know exactly what to do, how to touch him to excite him. Gregg had tried not to think about the men she'd known before him, but now...

"Maybe you should ask her about it, Greg," Snapper said, putting a consoling arm around his brother's drooping shoulders. "There's always a chance I'm talking about the wrong girl. But I had to warn you. I couldn't just let you go on making plans, deciding your future, if..." he hesitated. "Well, you know."

"Sure," Greg said bitterly. "I suppose I should thank you."

"No. There's no need for that. Just be sure, will you, before you take the big step."

"What do you suggest I do? Cruise around? Try to pick up my fiance'e?"

"Don't be so hard on yourself, Greg. Come on, we'd better go back inside. Remember, Mom made a cake for dessert."

"You go ahead," Greg shrugged off his brother's arm. "There's somebody I've got to see. Downtown."

Chapter Eight

Going Straight

The night was overcast, the roads as desolate as Greg's heart. Still, he drove aimlessly all over town, through neighborhoods he'd never seen before. The only place he didn't drive was downtown. Greg avoided the heart of Genoa City as if it were a no man's land. He didn't want to believe Snapper...and yet, as a lawyer, he couldn't get away from the fact that there was so much supporting evidence for his charges. Greg knew he could never marry Gwen now, until he found out the truth, and then...His mind stalled.

He'd been over the same territory a million times since Snapper's heart-to-heart talk. Still, he couldn't get past that final point—at least not until he talked to Gwen. Not until he heard her admit that she had been deceiving him, lying to him, tricking him.

Greg never went back home that night. At dawn he was still driving, too sick at heart even to recognize how tired he was. In a few hours Gwen would be coming to his office. Stopping at an all-night diner, he ordered coffee and tried to decide what to say to her. Should he accuse her outright and force her to prove her innocence? Wait for her to confess what she was? Or simply tell her that he hadn't meant what he'd said—that the wedding, the very idea of marriage, had been momentary madness on his part?

"Good morning, darling." Gwen sauntered into Greg's office, as familiar there as she was in her own apartment, and stopped short. "What happened to you?" she asked, her voice heavy with concern. "Do you feel all right? You look as if you died and were dug up." She started toward Greg's desk but his greeting stopped her abruptly in her tracks.

"Hi, Scarlet!" he said.

From the expression on Greg's face, Gwen realized instantly that all her dreams had just gone up in smoke. The smile froze on her lips, and she stopped as if she'd been slapped. Still, she wasn't ready to give up Greg. He was the only good thing that had ever happened to her, and she would fight to hold him to his promise. In her profession she had learned to counter all kinds of hostility from cruel, sadistic men. By comparison, Greg was as threatening as a baby.

"Do you have time to go out for coffee?" she asked. Once she'd regained her composure, she stooped over his desk and planted a kiss on the crown of his head, ignoring his unwelcome greeting.

"I've had coffee, thanks, but I have lots of time to listen." Greg's voice was tight, and his fingers clenched around the paperweight on his desk as if that pressure alone were holding him together. "Why don't you sit down and start at the beginning?"

"Sure," she said breezily, perching on the arm of the chair beside him. "What do you want to talk about?"

"Have you ever thought of trying the truth? It has a way of coming out eventually anyway," he added, the bitterness so keen Gwen could taste it.

"I don't know what you're talking about, darling." Gwen looked at him, her wide blue eyes as clear as mountain water. "You're my lawyer. You know I confide in you." Her voice held a teasing quality that annoyed Greg.

"Is that all I am?"

"I thought you were my fiancé, too, but at the moment you don't exactly sound like a loving husband-to-be."

"Did it ever occur to you that I might not like being lied to?"

"I have no idea what you're talking about, Greg. But it looks like I caught you at the wrong time," she said, still smiling. "Why don't I go now and try to come back later when you're feeling better?"

She stood up and swung her pocketbook over her shoulder, but his words stopped her retreat.

"That's exactly what you did, isn't it? You caught me—number one chump of the year, Greg Foster. There's a sucker born every day, and girls like you know just how to spot them."

"O.K., Greg." Gwen sat down heavily in the chair and studied her long scarlet nails intently. "You may as well say everything you've been thinking and get it off your chest. Girls like me can take it," she added, knowing there was no point in pretending any longer.

She was a fool to think she could hide what she was from Greg forever. Genoa City was too small a town. Either somebody had told Greg, or he had seen her. Either way, it didn't make any difference. Looking up, she saw the hesitation in his face, the confusion as if powerful emotions were battling each other.

"Go on," she said harshly, slipping into the tone she used on the streets. "Say it! Say it all!" She laughed jeeringly, knowing that the gig was up. "There ain't nothing I haven't heard before, buddy."

Although Gwen was making it easier for him by the change in her manner, Greg stared at her as if she were possessed. Some part of him had refused to believe it until that moment. "All this time you've been lying to me. You never had a job. You weren't working overtime every night. You were turning tricks—just like you did with me." His voice rose higher with every accusation until he was shouting at her.

"No!" Gwen cried. Even in his anger, the sharpness of her denial cut him off. "It was never like that with you...not even the first time."

"Then why did you lie to me?" Greg demanded.

"Because I was afraid. Why do you think? I didn't want to lose you."

"You should have trusted me enough to tell me."

"Sure, I can see it all now. If I said, 'Sorry, Greg, I can only see you afternoons because I have a night job. I'm a hooker. You can catch me any night at the corner of Broad and Chestnut Streets...' If I said that you never would have given me a chance."

"Instead, you never gave me one."

"Don't you see?" She looked up at him for the first time, her eyes dark and pleading. "I couldn't believe that anybody warm and decent and honest like you could ever care for me. And when you did...or at least you seemed to...I wanted to be the kind of girl you thought I was."

"Then why didn't you quit—go straight?" Although the challenge was still clear in his voice, her response had touched him and his accusations were softer now.

"I have to eat, same as everyone else, pay the damn rent...the whole bit. I don't know how to do anything else." She shrugged, knowing that it was useless to try to explain. Even now Gwen couldn't tell Greg everything. She couldn't tell him what it was like to owe her body and soul to Duke Stevens.

"But how could you make love to me, then leave and do the same thing with a dozen other men?" The pain in Greg's voice was so acute that Gwen ached to take him in her arms and comfort him the only way she knew how. But he wouldn't want her now—he'd never want her again.

"I told you. It was different." Her voice was so soft, he had to strain to hear her. "I didn't feel anything with the others. It was just a job, like working in a factory on the assembly line. They paid and I delivered. I wouldn't recognize any of them five minutes later. It had nothing to do with me," she insisted again. "It was a job—a rough, stinking, dirty job—but I had to survive. Can't you understand that?"

"You could have done something else," he persisted stubbornly. "Anything."

"Do you know what it's like to be desperate?" Gwen challenged, her eyes flashing suddenly. She wasn't going to apologize for herself anymore. She'd done what she'd had to do, and if Greg despised her for it, then what was the use of all this talk, all the questions, all the explanations? He'd never understand. "I was fifteen. I had three dollars in my pocket after paying for my bus ticket, and this was the end of the line. I slept in the bus station for two nights and ate candy bars until I began to stink and my face broke out. Then this guy came up to me—real smooth, a snappy dresser. He offered to put me up, give me some real food...I couldn't believe my luck. I thought he was really taken with me, that's what a kid I was. Regular farm hick, grass still sticking out of my ears," she laughed self-mockingly. "He said I was beautiful and he called me Scarlet. Scarlet! I should have guessed. He said he loved me and I was going to be his girl. Between one thing and another we began making it. He was the first, that's how green I was. I thought we'd get married, make beautiful babies, just like in the movies..."

Gwen shook her head as if, even now, she couldn't believe her own naiveté. "I really believed that—for a couple of weeks, anyway. He bought me sexy clothes and stockings and make-up. It was like Christmas, except the season was wrong. At least that's what I thought." She laughed harshly. "Then he told me he'd had a streak of bad luck. I had to help him out...pay my own way...just till he got back on his feet. When I told him I didn't know how to do anything except work on a farm, he laughed. 'Sure you do—you know how to hustle. Just make love the way I taught you and before you know it, you'll have mink coats and fancy cars...anything you want.'

"I didn't want to do it. I cried and begged and threatened to go back to sleeping in the bus station. But he wouldn't let me leave. He said he'd invested too much in me to let me walk out on him. I was stubborn, I guess, or maybe I was just plain scared. I tried to run away, but he caught me. He tied me up and beat me." Gwen related her horrifying story flatly, without a trace of emotion, as if she were telling Greg something that had happened to another girl. And in a way, she was. "He wouldn't give me anything to eat— just a glass of water. If I didn't do what he asked me to he'd beat me again. After a while hustling began to look good."

"Christ!" Greg muttered. He'd covered his face in his hands as Gwen talked, unable to look at her as she made her pathetic confession. He'd been so righteous, telling her she shouldn't have lied to him. Now he understood that the truth was sometimes worse.

"Do you know what it's like out on the street in the heat, the rain, the freezing cold? Having to go with every John who's got an extra twenty-dollar bill in his pocket? Usually they want something kinky—something they wouldn't dare ask their wives to do. But since they're paying, anything goes." Gwen leaned her head back against the chair and shut her eyes, as if she could make it all go away.

"I know what you're thinking, Greg," she said. "You're thinking that I could have stopped any time I wanted. But it isn't that easy. Once I began hustling, I started to take drugs—just to get me through the night. That's what I'd tell myself. But then a little wasn't enough, so I took more—harder stuff—and before I even knew it, I was hooked. Trapped. Because every dollar I made went to pay for my habit, and the more tricks I turned, the more drugs I needed."

Opening her eyes, Gwen sat up and slung her purse over her shoulder again. "Now that you know the whole sordid story of Scarlet Sherman," she said harshly, "you can come down to Broad and Chestnut any night you've got an extra twenty. I'll even give you a discount—for old time's sake," she added in her toughest street voice as she stood up.

Greg remained as he had throughout the whole narration, his face buried in his hands. When he didn't look up, she blew him a kiss and headed for the door.

"So long, lover boy," she called over her shoulder. "Maybe I'll see you downtown sometime."

As long as she played it tough, Gwen wouldn't break down. She'd learned how to harden herself so that she didn't feel anything. But at the slightest hint of tenderness, the facade would crumble.

Listening to her heels click across the office floor, each step taking her out of his life forever, Greg wrestled with his conflicting emotions. How could he reconcile the girl he loved with the hooker whose hopeless story he'd just heard?

How could he let her go back to more of the same—more abuse, degradation, abasement?

"Wait, Gwen!" he called, as he reached the door.

"Another time, O.K." She shook her head. "I'll give you a rain check."

"No!" he insisted.

Before she could open the door, he was beside her. Gwen sensed his approach before she saw him—saw the pity, the grief, the tenderness reflected in his face and tried to get away.

"Don't touch me," she warned, but it was too late.

Greg's hands were on her shoulders, turning her around. "Jesus, Gwen, I'm sorry. I had no idea," he murmured into her crown of flaming hair. Tears glistened in his eyes as his arms encircled her, holding her close.

Gwen could stand up against everything — except a loving touch. The minute she felt Greg's arms around her, her toughness abandoned her. "Let me go," she begged, but Greg was pressing her head against his shoulder.

"It's all right, Gwen. You don't have to fight me too. I want to help you, if you'll just let me," he insisted. "I can't let you go back out there. I can't even bear to think of it."

"You're too good for me, Greg. I've known it all along." Her voice broke and the disappointment, the discouragement, the unbearable feeling of oss overwhelmed her. The control she'd been holding onto so tightly broke and, surrendering to his arms, she sank against him, her body shaking convulsively with sobs. "I'm just what I am. That's all I'll ever be," she cried through the flood of tears that streaked down her cheeks, soaking through the shoulder of Greg's jacket.

He held her, stroking her hair and letting her weep, until gradually her sobs subsided and the stream of tears slowed. "You don't have to go back to that life," he said, when she was quiet in his arms. "You can give it up. Go straight."

"It's too late." She shook her head disconsolately. "It's all I'm good for now."

"You *can* stop, Gwen, if you really want to," Greg persisted.

"Don't you understand?" She began to cry again. "I wanted to stop even before I began, and look at me!"

"You look beautiful to me. You always will," Greg soothed. "And you can go straight, if you'll only try. I'll help you."

She looked up at him, her long, coppery lashes shimmering with tears. "Do you mean it, Greg? Do you really think I can?"

Wiping away a tear that had spilled over the brim of her eye, he smiled down at her. "I believe in you, Gwen, but that's not enough. You have to believe in yourself, too."

She didn't ask him if he would still marry her. Gwen knew that that was too much to hope for now. An impossible dream—that's all it had ever been. But if Greg would help her, maybe—just maybe—she could start again. A glimmer of hope shone through the darkness that was her life. "If you'll stay with me, just for a while, then I'll do it. I'll stop hustling. I'll start over again," she vowed, "but I can't do it alone."

"You won't be alone, Gwen. I promise," Greg said. And before he could pull away, her lips had found his and were sealing the vow they had just exchanged with a kiss sweeter than any he had ever tasted.

Stuart Brooks's voice sounded too controlled over the interoffice phone. "If you have a few minutes, Brad, would you come into my office. I want to speak to you about something—something very personal," he added.

"Of course, sir," Brad answered quickly. "I'll be right in."

Stuart Brooks had just returned from New York. The weeklong vacation he'd originally planned had been extended to a month—an unprecedented length of time for him to be away from the newspaper. If the city editor knew why Brooks was away so long, he didn't divulge the information to any of his reporters. And when Brad questioned Laurie about her parents' prolonged absence, she brushed aside his concern with vague answers. Now, seated across the desk from Brooks, Brad was shocked by the change in him. He seemed to have aged ten years in a single month. A gray patina coated his face; black circles outlined his eyes; and the vitality that had fired the *Genoa City Herald*, making it a prize-winning newspaper, seemed to have disappeared entirely.

"Are you all right, sir?" Brad asked with obvious concern.

"I suppose so," Brooks answered, "apart from being tired and worried. Jennifer and I have been in New York...I don't know how much Laurie has told you already."

"Nothing at all," Brad said. "Actually, she's been very vague about your whole trip."

Brooks's eyes narrowed as he focused intently on Brad's face. "That's strange," he replied, as much to himself as to Brad. "You see, we went to New York for the final concert in Leslie's tour. Only we never heard it." He paused and inhaled sharply as if he were afraid he might lose control before he finished speaking. "Leslie disappeared from her hotel room. Her manager had called us the day before to say she was depressed and acting strangely. We hoped our visit would cheer her up. Instead, we never got to see her. She simply disappeared," he repeated again, shaking his head as if he still couldn't believe what had happened. "Of course we alerted the police, offered rewards, hired private detectives... everything."

The color had drained from Brad's face as Brooks spoke. "And where did you find her?" he asked anxiously.

"We haven't, yet. She vanished without a trace. I was hoping you could answer that question, Brad." Brooks toyed with the lead weight on his desk. "I don't mean to pry into your private affairs—even though they do involve two of my daughters—but Jennifer is convinced that Leslie's depression began after her first concert in Detroit. It seems that she was very disappointed because you didn't go to it."

"But we had broken up months before that," Brad reminded him.

"It might have been over with you, Brad, but Leslie hadn't given up hope," Brooks answered, his voice tight. "That's why she sent you the invitation. I know you didn't respond to it. Still, I was wondering if you'd had any other communication from her since then."

"Hold on." Brad put up a warning hand, but Brooks misunderstood the gesture.

"I can't force you to answer me," he began.

"It's not that," Brad interrupted. "You've got it all wrong, sir. Leslie never sent me an invitation. I was hoping she would..." His voice trailed off.

"But she *did*," Brooks insisted. "She told her mother, and when you didn't show up..."

"Nothing could have kept me away if I thought for a second Leslie wanted me to be there."

"Jennifer says it's the only thing in the world she *did* want. She played like an angel. The audience gave her a standing ovation. The critics raved. But she didn't care about any of it. When she didn't hear from you, she became depressed. I guess it just kept escalating, until she couldn't handle it any longer by the time she reached New York. God only knows what happened to her there. I'm not accusing you, Brad..."

"But I *am* accusing *you*," Brad burst out. Once he'd recovered from Brooks's stunning news, Brad's initial shock turned to anger. "Why didn't one of you say something then, when Leslie first became depressed?"

"It was a little awkward," Brooks admitted. "Because that was right about the time you and Laurie announced your engagement."

"Did Leslie know about that?" Brad asked tensely.

Brooks shook his head. "Neither Jennifer nor I had the heart to tell her. She was still so broken up about you."

"None of it makes any sense," Brad muttered, running his fingers through his thick black hair.

"Laurie said," he began, then stopped himself abruptly. Suddenly his confusion was clearing, scrambled pieces of the puzzle falling into place. "Laurie said," he started again slowly, deliberately, "that I was standing in Leslie's way. That's why I let her go. And when she started the tour, Laurie said Leslie was happier than she'd ever been. A brilliant career, a new world was opening to her. She was lost to me forever."

With each word Brad spoke, Brooks felt as if there was a weight inside him growing heavier and heavier. "You weren't standing in Leslie's way, Brad. She loved you. But maybe," he ground out each word as if it were painful to speak, "Leslie was standing in her sister's way."

The two men stared at each other across the wide polished desk, the same thought uniting them, choking Brad with a murderous rage, filling Brooks with a pervasive sadness. No matter what difficult times his family was called upon to face, Stuart Brooks had always believed that they would at least be true to each other. His four daughters would stand united, never faltering in their love for each other. That thought had sustained him through Chris's rape, elopement, and miscarriage; through Laurie's long absence in Paris; through the painful breakup of Leslie's engagement. Now even that had dissolved like a puff of smoke.

"I request an immediate—and indefinite—leave of absence, sir," Brad was saying. Although outwardly he still appeared calm, he was gripping the arms of the chair so tightly that his knuckles were white. "I'm going to New York and I'm not coming back until I find Leslie—no matter how long that takes."

In spite of his fear for Leslie, in spite of all the unthinkable things that could have happened to a fragile, vulnerable girl alone in New York, Brad felt alive for the first time in months. So much precious time had been wasted, so much needless pain given and received. But he vowed to himself that he would make it up to Leslie when he found her again—even if it took him a lifetime. And he refused to even consider the possibility that she was lost forever.

Stuart Brooks stared out the window in brooding silence, considering Brad's request and his own divided family. "What about Laurie?" he asked, finally breaking the silence between them.

"What about Laurie?" was all Brad could trust himself to answer.

Chapter Nine

Love and Betrayal

For the third straight day Gwen lay in bed pretending to be sick, trying to formulate a plan of escape. She didn't know what else to do and still keep her promise to Greg. There was so much she hadn't told Greg when she made her confession. So much she couldn't tell him even now. Gwen could never tell him that Duke Stevens still owned her. That he controlled her mind and body, possessed her through fear and brutality, that she belonged to him, was dependent on him for whatever she needed: clothes, food, drugs. Every dollar she made, she had to turn over to him.

How could she tell Greg that she was part of Duke's stable? That he picked up girls—lost, frightened, confused, homeless runaways like her—and took possession of them until they had no will, no power left to refuse him.

Duke Stevens. Once he'd seemed like a god to Gwen. Now he was the incarnation of evil: a devil. The only way she could keep her promise to Greg was to break away from Duke. But how? For three days Gwen had kept off the street, feigning illness, but she couldn't deceive Duke for long. If he even suspected that she was trying to beat him out of a night's work...

Gwen never had a chance to finish the thought. Because just at that moment she heard the door open, and Duke loomed in the doorway, a vicious smile curling back his lips, revealing two rows of small, even teeth. Although he was of slight, wiry build, Duke's power gave him the illusion of superior size. His complexion was pasty white and pockmarked. His eyes were small and of such a pale shade of blue that they appeared almost translucent; his black hair was combed in a thick Afro. High-heeled lizard boots and a big Stetson hat added to the illusion of size.

Thumbs hooked under the silver-studded belt of his tight black jeans, he stood in the doorway, smiling at Gwen, not saying a word. Instinctively, she huddled deeper into the bed, pulling the blankets tighter around her, trying to find her voice. Her fear was so great she could taste it.

"Hi, Duke," she managed to stammer. "What are you doing here?"

"I came to see how you were feeling, Scarlet. There's talk on the street that you're going to pull a fast one on Duke. I've even heard that you've found yourself a fancy lawyer and that you're figuring on skipping out on me without so much as a 'thank you' for all I've done for you, or even a goodbye kiss. That's sort of ungrateful now, don't you think, Scarlet?"

His tone was friendly—frighteningly so—and

Gwen trembled in terror, afraid of what was coming next. She hadn't had a pop all day for Greg's sake, and her body was already bathed in a cold sweat from the withdrawal. If she'd had something to help her, even a little fix, she might have been able to stand up to Duke. But as it was she collapsed, crying and begging him.

"It's not like that, Duke. I'd never try to leave you. You're the best. There ain't nobody like you. You're real good to me." She stumbled through a litany of praise, at the same time trying to protect herself from the blow she was sure would come.

"You want to know what I think, Scarlet?" He crossed the room in three quick strides and yanked the bedclothes off her. "I think there ain't nothing wrong with you that a good, healthy beating won't cure."

"No, Duke! It's not like that. Honest, it's not!" Gwen cowered, curling her legs up into a fetal position and hugging her breasts in anticipation of the blow. If she just took it and didn't fight back, maybe he'd only hit her once, Gwen prayed.

But Duke wasn't in the mood for a light punishment. Gwen had dared to defy him. If he let her get away with it, every other girl in his stable would think she could too. And besides, he enjoyed it; he took a sadistic pleasure in keeping his women in line. Grabbing Gwen's leg he yanked it straight and pulled a leather thong from his pocket.

"No, Duke!" she screamed, knowing what was coming next. "I'm sick. Honest I am...I didn't do nothing."

His fist struck out and caught her just below the eye, silencing her. "I'm just warming up, Scarlet," he grinned savagely, grabbing her other leg. "We'll see how much your lawyer-honey wants you after I'm through," he laughed.

When she was bound on the bed, he pulled off his studded belt and went to work. The first lash snapped across her mouth when she opened it to scream. The second cracked across her body. After a while, Gwen didn't bother to count.

"I want to see you out there tonight, even if you don't turn a single trick," Duke warned when he was finished. Giving Gwen a final savage crack across her face that sent her head whipsawing to show he meant business, Duke untied her bonds, menace clear in his every motion.

"How can I go out looking like this?" Gwen whimpered helplessly, touching the ugly purple bruise under her eye where Duke's fist had made contact with her cheekbone, and her split lip which had already begun to swell, making her speech sound slurred. "Nobody will come near me."

"If you're not on the street, I'll be back. You've already cost me plenty, faking you were sick for three days just because some fancy lawyer told you to. If he wants to help you again, next time tell him to come downtown and start paying for what you've been giving away free. Because you're going to have to work your ass off to make up for all you gave him. I figure you must owe me a grand easy. And if you don't want to pay up, then I might just get it into my head to go collect from him."

Duke considered taking her then—just to show her who was boss, whom she belonged to—not that he wanted her, but because he knew it would debase her more. Then he thought better of it. He didn't want her blood to dirty his new shirt. Instead, he took a packet of white powder out of his pocket and dropped it on the table beside her bed.

"You're going to need that to get out there long enough to even the score with me. And remember, Scarlet," he added over his shoulder, "I'll be watching you out there. I'll be watching real close, and the next time I won't touch you. I have a better idea. I'll pay a little call on your lawyer friend. 'Foster' his name is, isn't it?"

Duke laughed with malicious enjoyment at the stricken look on Gwen's bruised, swollen face. "He's a pretty boy, ain't he? But he won't be for long when I get through with him."

Gwen waited until she heard the door slam and she was sure Duke was gone; then she fingered the packet he had left for her. Her body ached so much from his beating that she didn't think she could get as far as the bathroom to retch. But the white powder would deaden the pain—and deaden her when she dragged herself out on the street that night. It would just be one more thing that Greg never had to know, she told herself.

Jill Foster stood at the French doors, watching the sheets of rain slash down into the Chancellors' formal gardens. Except for the occasional eruptions of thunder, the house was as silent as a haunted mansion. Most of the staff had gone home for the evening, and those few who remained were closeted together in the kitchen playing cards. Kay and Phillip had gone to the country club for the harvest moon ball, and Jill had decided to use the quiet time to catch up on Kay's correspondence.

Watching the rain, Jill thought about how handsome Phillip had looked in his tuxedo. Her shoulder still burned where he touched her as he went out, gently reminding her not to work too late. Even so, the time had gotten away from her, and now the rain was so heavy she would have to wait until it let up. The Fosters didn't live in the same part of town as the Chancellors, and it was a long trek for Jill—especially on a dark, stormy night. After calling her mother to say she'd be late, Jill curled up on the sofa to wait out the rain.

She didn't mind, really. Alone in the Chancellors' elegant home she could allow her fantasies to run wild. Sitting in the soft lamplight, her shoes kicked off, her feet tucked up on the goldenrod brocade pillow, it almost seemed like her own house. Since he had kissed her in the cabana, Jill had rarely allowed herself to be alone with Phillip. Yet the explosive emotion between them, as if they were live electric wires, only continued to heighten. The silent communion they shared was even stronger than a conventional romance, because each moment they denied themselves only served to fuel their desires. All they could exchange was a furtive look, a longing smile, a whispered word, an accidental touch. But these small contacts kept their dream alive. One day Kay would be well again, and then...

Alone in the house, Jill surrendered to her

most cherished dream. She, not Kay, was attending the country club ball on Phillip's arm. Closing her eyes, she saw herself transformed as perfectly as Cinderella. Her dress was a gossamer cloud of pink chiffon that floated around her, baring her milky shoulders, hugging her narrow waist. The fragrance of some exotic perfume, like jasmine, lingered on her shoulders, and when Phillip swept her up in his arms to dance the scent wafted toward him, intoxicating him with desire. Together they glided round and round the dance floor. Around them on all sides club members murmured what a glorious couple they made—'such a welcome change from Kay.' But Phillip and Jill never heard a word. Never heard anything except the music of the orchestra that was making their bodies waltz as one, the music of their own hearts that was singing a wondrous song of love.

Jill sighed and snuggled deeper into the couch. The rain had stopped, but her dream would go on forever. She would never stop dancing, stop holding, stop loving Phillip Chancellor.

"Jill!" She felt a soft tap on her shoulder and heard his voice calling her name.

"Mmmmm," she sighed in her sleep, "I'd love to dance with you again." Her arms curled up around his neck, drawing him down to her as she brushed her cheek against his dreamily.

"Jill!" he repeated, trying to shake her. "Wake up. You must be dreaming." Although he unlocked her arms from his neck and held her wrists so that she couldn't embrace him again, his heart was beating dangerously fast.

Sleepily opening her eyes, Jill yawned and stretched sensuously, making his body leap with desire. It had been a disastrous night, which was why they were home early. Kay must have been drinking secretly all day, because the moment they arrived at the club she began creating a scene. At first she was just rude and demanding, threatening the bartender when he tried to dissuade her from another drink. But as the evening progressed she grew more outrageous, complaining for all to hear that her husband was a eunuch, and offering herself provocatively to every man at the dance.

Now though, gazing down at Jill, Phillip's body tensed with desire. The hideous evening paled, and all he could think of was how thoroughly he wanted to know her, to love her, to possess her.

"Phillip!" Jill murmured, yearning toward him. Her dream had been so vivid, in that netherworld between sleep and wakefulness, that she couldn't tell where one ended and the other began.

Forgetting all caution, all promises, he pulled her into his arms and crushed her against his chest, whispering her name again and again.

"Phillip! Where have you gone now, and where's the damn gin bottle?" Kay's belligerent voice in the hall just outside the door stopped them, freezing them into statues.

For an instant longer, Phillip clung to Jill, then he released her quickly and turned away without a word. "Go to bed, Kay," he shouted huskily. "You've made enough of a spectacle of yourself for one night." Going out into the hall, he saw that she had already started up the stairs, half crawling, half pulling herself along the bannister, probably to dredge up a fresh bottle she had stashed away in her unending store.

Disgusted, he turned away from the sight of his wife and found Jill framed in the doorway behind him. "I'll drive you home," he said, more gently. "You shouldn't work this late at night. It's dangerous."

"I wasn't working. I was waiting for the rain to stop. I must have fallen asleep," she apologized.

"It was a nasty night," he shook his head bleakly at the memory, "and I don't mean just the weather."

"I'm sorry."

He sighed. "I guess I should be used to it. But I'm not," he confessed. "I'm just tired of it—especially now, because I want you so much."

"I was dreaming we were dancing," Jill smiled up at him. "I was like Cinderella at the ball, only I didn't have to look for my Prince Charming. I had already found him."

"We will dance, Jill. . .one day," he promised. For a long moment he stood looking at her, loving her with his eyes, his heart, his hopes. Then, with a supreme effort of will, he wrenched himself away. "The car's still outside. I told the chauffeur to take the rest of the night off, so I'll drive you myself."

"You don't have to do that, Phillip," she began to protest, but he had already started out into the damp, black night.

With a glance up the stairs where Kay had disappeared, Jill followed him, wondering how much longer she could work for the Chancellors and still trust herself with Phillip. A few moments before on the couch, she had forgotten everything except how much she wanted him. It would be so easy to forget again.

"Come on!" Phillip was calling to her, and opening the car door. She hurried after his voice.

In the darkness Jill stumbled on the gravel drive and lurched against him. "I'm sorry. I guess I'm still half-asleep," she began to apologize. But his arms had already closed around her and his lips encompassed hers, muffling her words.

"Jill, oh Jill," he murmured, smoothing back her hair, caressing her face with urgent hands. "I want you so much. I need you. Say yes, darling, just once. Being so close, yet not having you, not even touching you, is torture for me."

"I love you, Phil," she whispered into the black night.

"Tell me again, and again," he murmured as his lips closed over hers a second time, his hands roaming urgently over her back.

All restraint was lost, all their best intentions consumed in the fire of their hunger. Their desire for each other was so great, it was like an irresistible tidal wave sweeping over everything that stood in its way, until there was nothing left except a man and a woman and a passion that demanded to be answered.

Kay stumbled out onto the second-floor balcony, a tumbler of gin clutched in her hand as if it were a lifeline. The rain had stopped and the first stars had come out, sprinkling the black sky with specks of light. She leaned against the wall, drinking thirstily, only dimly aware of the dampness against her back.

"The hell with you, Phillip Chancellor. The hell with you all," she swore into the glass. Staggering to the railing, she leaned over, feeling the waves of nausea and dizziness sweep over her. She needed another drink to dispel them. But just as she started back into the house to empty the fifth of gin, she stopped suddenly and peered down at the lawn below. Even through the haze of liquor and darkness, she was sure her eyes weren't deceiving her.

Phillip was crossing the lawn just beneath, carrying something in his arms as carefully as if it were a cherished treasure. She could see arms wrapped around his neck and bare legs dangling over his arm. In spite of all the liquor she had consumed, the sight had a sobering effect. It was one thing for Phillip to deny her. It was quite another for him to take one of their servants in her place. She watched his figure disappear toward the cabanas with mounting rage.

Dashing the glass over the balcony in her fury, Kay was torn inside. For years she had used the stableboys for sex because Phillip had refused her. But she had never rejected him. A few moments later, a ghostly apparition could be seen crossing the lawn, following the path that Phillip and Jill had taken. Though barefoot, Kay was still dressed in the long, flowing ecru gown she'd worn to the country club ball. Stealthily, she crept up to the high cabana window and peered in. But she wasn't prepared for the sight that met her eyes. Her face turned a deathly pallor, and she gripped the windowsill to keep from fainting. She'd expected to see one of the housemaids. Instead, she saw Jill Foster wrapped in Phillip's arms.

Kay knew she should turn away. But some demonic force held her at the window. It was one thing to watch a sex scene on a movie screen. It was quite another to watch your husband making love to another woman.

Jill's body was beautiful, more sexy than hers had ever been, she thought with a pang of jealousy. She had a voluptuousness, a sensuality that her own angular body had always lacked. Was that what Phillip wanted, what she could never give him? Kay wondered bitterly. By now the effects of the gin had worn off as if she'd had water, and in its place was a cold, implacable loathing.

She had loved Phillip and trusted Jill, and now, together, they were betraying her. Like someone under a hypnotic spell, she stood watching them, every second seared into her memory forever more. And with the bitter vision printed indelibly in her mind, she vowed never to rest until she had destroyed them both.

Chapter Ten

To Forgive Is Divine

Greg knew he shouldn't, yet he couldn't help himself. He wanted to trust Gwen. He wanted to believe in the promise she had made to him. Still, he found himself cruising the downtown area, each loop he made growing smaller and smaller until he was coasting down Broad Street. Two blocks from the corner of Chestnut, he slowed to a crawl. What would he do if Gwen were out there? Could he just drive by...and if he stopped?

There was no point in imagining what he would do. Because as the car inched along, Greg saw the flaming torch of her hair burnished by a streetlight on the corner. A burly man stood in front of her, blocking her face from Greg's view. By the time he pulled up to them, they had started to walk away arm-in-arm.

For an instant he sat motionless, the motor idling, and watched the sway of Gwen's hips as she moved further away from him. Her kiss had been so sweet when she sealed her promise to him that he couldn't believe it was a lie—another lie. Yet his eyes were not deceiving him. The John's arm moved along Gwen's back to clutch her proprietorially.

Choking back the fury and the nausea that churned inside him at the sight, Greg pulled to a stop, brakes squealing, and raced down the street after them. At the sound of the heavy footsteps behind her, Gwen wheeled around, fear leaping from her eyes, and stopped dead.

"Greg!" her lips formed his name, but no sound came out. They faced each other, staring with passionate intensity, one filled with shame, the other overcome with fury.

"What are you doing here?" Gwen gasped, finding her voice at last.

"That's what I should be asking you." Greg spat out the words contemptuously. "But it's pretty obvious, isn't it? You're doing what you want to do—what you like to do best, aren't you? Poor little helpless Gwen," he sneered, bitterness turning him cruel. "And I was dumb enough to fall for your line. You must have been laughing at me every second."

Although Gwen's heart was breaking, she couldn't let Greg see that she cared. Somewhere in the shadows, Duke would be watching them. Watching Greg. "You shouldn't have come down here. It's too dangerous," she tried to warn him in a whisper. But Greg was too consumed by anger to understand her message.

"Come on, babe. I'm paying for you, not this joker." The John lurched drunkenly for her.

"Steady, Jack!" She pulled away from him, snapping her gum at his leering face. "We've got all night, so what's your hurry?"

Rigid with rage and disillusionment, Greg stared at her—at the garish, provocative clothing that hugged her figure as tightly as his arms had, at the thick make-up that hid the evidence of Duke's beating. "How could I ever have thought I loved you! You're cheap! That's all you'll ever be. That's all you want to be," he charged furiously. "You like it, Gwen. Admit it, damn you, you like it."

For a last, longing moment, Gwen looked at Greg and saw all that might have been...that could never be. Then she shrugged and slipped her hand through the impatient John's arm.

"Beats working any day, that's what I always say." She forced herself to speak in a loud, crude voice. "Want to tag along, honey? Three's not a crowd with Scarlet. It's a frigging party."

Sick with revulsion and heartache, Greg turned on his heels and started walking away, without a thought, a purpose, a destination—just wanting to put as much distance as possible between himself and Gwen. He'd loved her, damn her. He'd loved the girl he thought she was—the flaming-haired beauty named Gwen that he'd invented on a rainy summer day in a hushed pine grove. He hadn't lost Chris because he'd never truly possessed her. And now he hadn't lost Gwen, because she'd never existed except in his imagination.

Gwen watched him go, her eyes flooding with tears, until his figure grew small, like a miniature, and the John tugged on her arm.

"Come on, babe, you're with me, remember? He's just one of the crazies roaming around these days. Forget him."

"One of the crazies...and I'm crazy about him," she murmured brokenly to herself.

"You and me—we're going to have ourselves a good time."

"Sure," Gwen sobbed. "A helluva time! Anything you want, and it's on the house. What the hell! Nothing matters anymore."

A rare and blessed peace prevailed in the emergency room of the Genoa City Hospital. Usually the place was rushed and overcrowded, nurses and interns functioning nonstop on quarts of black, inky coffee and an overflow of adrenalin. But for once the waiting room was empty and the ambulance sirens quiet. Snapper Foster propped his feet up on the desk in the staff office and leaned back, munching on a jelly doughnut. Just one more night to go, he thought, then he'd be back on day duty for the rest of the month, weary but happy. That meant he'd see a lot more of his wife.

Since Chris had agreed to a trial reunion, Snapper had never been happier. He wasn't sure why. Maybe realizing how much he'd almost lost made him appreciate his marriage more. Or maybe he and Chris had both done some much-needed growing up. Whatever the reason, Snapper and Chris had never been better together. Snapper had begun his residency at the hospital, and Chris had gone back to college to get her degree. They were both busy—too busy to think about having another baby yet—but now they had time, years and years together to plan the family they both dreamed of. Even his father-in-law, Stuart Brooks, seemed to accept him more, Snapper thought, pleased with the direction his life was taking. After so many obstacles, so much stumbling, he could look at himself and his family with pride.

In another two years, if his luck held, he'd be able to give his mother enough money each month so that she wouldn't have to go on working. His sister, Jill, seemed secure and satisfied as Kay Chancellor's girl Friday. The only cloud in this picture he was painting was Greg. In spite of their differences Snapper loved his brother deeply, and unreasonably blamed himself for allowing Greg to get involved with Gwen Sherman. He should have protected his brother, taken more of an interest in whom he was dating. But it had never occurred to him that his idealistic, upright kid brother would get involved with a prostitute.

Finishing his doughnut in a single oversized bite, Snapper stretched and went over to the sink to wash his hands. The distant screech of an ambulance siren was growing closer. With any luck, he thought, as he started back toward the nurses' station, it would be his last case of the night.

"Got a bad one for you," the driver was saying as he wheeled the stretcher in. "One of the hookers who hangs out down on Broad Street, her landlord said. Looks like she O.D.'d— intentionally or not, who can say?" He shrugged, as much as if to say 'it's all in a night's work.'" "We did the best we could...at least she's still breathing."

Snapper took one look at the clear, white face

as smooth and still as marble, and the mass of red hair that encircled it as bright as a halo, and swore under his breath. "Did you get her name, Mac?" he asked the driver, sure of the answer he was going to receive.

"The name's Sherman—Gwen Sherman. Looks to be a kid, not much more than twenty, but she's had it rough all right. Wait till you see her body."

Once Gwen was settled in one of the small emergency room cubicles receiving transfusions and oxygen, Snapper began his examination with infinite gentleness, shocked and frightened by what he found.

For the hospital records, a female patient named Gwen Sherman had taken an overdose of heroin and turned on the gas as well—a double guarantee of death, he guessed. But the landlord had smelled the gas in time. For Dr. Snapper Foster, personally, the case was much more complicated. His examination revealed lacerations that covered three-quarters of the girl's body. Although they had begun to heal, in places the wounds were still raw and tender to the touch. Someone had beaten Gwen Sherman—and beaten her badly. Looking at her cut, battered body, Snapper couldn't believe that his brother could do such a thing—no matter how angry he was. And yet, Greg had been in love with Gwen. She'd been deceiving him from the beginning, leading him on, lying to him. What if in an overpowering rage Greg had lost control of himself? Everything in Snapper, everything that he knew about his brother, made him reject the possibility. Then he remembered how Greg had challenged him over Chris and the vicious fight they'd had.

His face as pale as Gwen's own, Snapper sat down on the straight chair beside her bed. He would have to wait until she regained consciousness—wait to find out the truth about his brother, no matter how long it took.

Sometime in the early morning, just after the sun rose, Gwen began to stir. At first her eyelids fluttered, then slowly opened. Dazed and weak, she looked around her, trying to figure out what had happened, where she was. Seeing her stir, Snapper went to her bedside and took her pulse.

"Who are you?" she asked feebly, still searching for something familiar to hold onto.

"Dr. Foster," he answered, offering her a sip of water. "You've had a pretty rough time, but I think you're going to be all right, Gwen, if you start taking better care of yourself."

Gwen stared up at him, pain etched in her huge blue eyes. She'd only heard one word that he said, and she repeated it vacantly. "Foster. Foster. Greg..." she whispered, and the tears welled in her eyes as she remembered. Remembered it all—the shattering confrontation with Greg; the crazed, debasing night with the John who turned out to be as brutal as Duke; and finally, the moment she'd stumbled home, barely able to walk, taken the rest of the white powder and turned on the gas.

"Why didn't you let me die? I want to die!" She tried to scream at Snapper, but she only had the strength to cry like a baby.

"Gwen," he said, still holding her hand and stroking it soothingly. "If you tell me what happened to you, I'll try to help you."

"No," she turned away from him. "Just let me die, please."

"I can't. I'm a doctor. My job is to help you live, not let you die. But there's another reason I want to help you, Gwen." Although he inhaled sharply, steeling himself for whatever would come, Snapper kept his voice low and comforting. "Greg Foster is my brother. I have to know if he...if he did any of this to you. If he hurt you, beat you..."

"Greg..." Gwen began to weep, terrible sobs wracking her body like a storm tossing the waves at sea.

"I know how Greg felt about you," Snapper pressed. "He loved you, but he was also very angry with you."

"Greg is good," Gwen sobbed, sad accusing eyes denying everything Snapper had feared. "He never even hit me. He loved me, he forgave me, he was going to help me go straight. But I couldn't. I couldn't," she sobbed.

Snapper waited until she was calmer, afraid of tiring her too much. Then he began to question her again. "Somebody was pretty mad with you to beat you up the way he did. Your body is covered with lacerations and it looks as if you've either been raped or badly abused. If Greg didn't do it..."

"No, not Greg," she insisted, her breath coming in short, labored gasps. "It was my... Duke beat me up, and he was going to beat up Greg too if I didn't go back on the street. That's why I went. I promised Greg I wouldn't but..." A wild, frenzied look came into Gwen's eyes, and she grasped Snapper's hand, clinging to it. "Greg doesn't know about Duke. Promise me you won't tell him," she begged. "Promise me you won't tell Greg anything. Duke will kill him. I know he will. He'll do anything. Promise me..."

Gwen's grip slackened, and her head fell back as she lost consciousness again.

Cursing himself for pressing her so much, Snapper buzzed for the nurse and swiftly began a new transfusion. Barking out sharp, curt orders, he worked furiously to save the life that was gradually slipping away from him. What if Gwen died at his hands? What would he tell Greg? After she had been beaten, prostituted herself, and attempted suicide—all to save Greg— Snapper couldn't let her die. He would never forgive himself—and neither would Greg.

From the few, barely coherent words she had sobbed out, Snapper could imagine vividly what had happened. However she earned her living, he thought, Gwen Sherman had courage and heart. Although she had asked him to keep her secret, Snapper knew that some promises were meant to be broken.

To a casual passerby the man seated in the wing chair in the hotel lobby might have been an actor or a TV celebrity. His dark, brooding looks made him stand out from any crowd. But a closer observer would note the anxiety lines etched on his handsome face, the tension marked by a tightness around his mouth, the discouragement reflected in his eyes.

Brad Elliot had been in New York for weeks searching for Leslie. He had walked virtually every mile in Manhattan; talked with dozens of policemen; interviewed Leslie's manager, stage-hands at the recital hall where she practiced and, individually, the entire staff of her hotel. He had followed up every lead the private detectives uncovered, and even visited the city morgue, staring morosely at the unclaimed corpses of all the Jane Does in New York City. And in every instance he had come up empty-handed.

The strain was beginning to show, making Brad restless and irritable. A grown woman doesn't disappear from New York City without a trace—and yet that was exactly what Leslie had apparently done. If she were dead, her body should have turned up by now. If she were hurt, she would have been treated at one of the city hospitals—he had checked them all. And if she had run away, where would she go? Not home to Genoa City because he was there. But where else? Chicago, where they had first made love? Paris, like her sister, Laurie?

Brad's face hardened at the thought of Laurie. Although she was his fiancée, he had left Genoa City without a word to her. He had been so totally deceived by her, he couldn't trust himself even to speak to her again. Now, waiting impatiently at his hotel, Brad forced Laurie out of his mind with the same single-minded determination that she had forced herself into his life, destroying her sister in the process.

His eyes wandered around the lobby, looking for the detective who was scheduled to meet him there with yet another lead to pursue—probably to another dead end. Although Stuart Brooks was paying a fortune to the best private investigative agency in the city to solve his daughter's case, the results so far had been dismal...and both time and hope were running out.

On another occasion Brad would have enjoyed the hotel. It was an old-fashioned establishment, the famed haunt of writers and pundits a generation ago, located on a dimly-lit side street a short walk from Times Square. Just across the street was an equally famous, equally low-key literary magazine, and down the block was a prestigious Ivy League university club. Classy company, Brad thought. The venerable hotel had made few concessions to the space age. Instead of the expanses of glass, chrome, and greenery that gleamed in the new, streamlined hotels, comfortable, overstuffed sofas and easy chairs were clustered in the lobby, arranged to facilitate the fine though vanishing art of civilized conversation,. In the afternoons cocktails were served there as if it were someone's living room, and waiters passed around silver trays of hot and cold canapés.

A short man with a shiny bald pate and heavy black-rimmed glasses pushed his way into the lobby. Wearing a green duffle coat and carrying a bulging briefcase, he looked more like a salesman than the movie image of the trench-coated private eye, but Brad recognized him immediately and waved him over. In the weeks that he had been in New York, the two men had developed a mutual, though somewhat grudging, respect for one another. Mike Kearney thought Brad expected miracles. And for his part, Brad thought that if Mike had worked eighteen hours on the case, it should have been twenty.

"What have you got this time?" Brad asked wearily. He had learned not to get his hopes up no matter how promising the lead sounded. The odds were they'd come up against just another blank wall.

"Not much," Mike warned. "It's a long shot, but everything's worth exploring, right?"

"Let's hear it," Brad said, understanding that the detective was trying to protect himself against another failure.

"It seems like a couple of rookie cops picked up a young woman roaming around Central Park in the rain one night around the time we're talking about. The report didn't show up in the police blotter before because the two cops were so green they botched up the whole procedure and the report just surfaced. It had been misplaced or misfiled. Who knows?" he shrugged. "It might be worth a shot."

"What name did the girl give?" Brad asked. "The cops must have gotten that right at least."

"Actually, that's the funny part. I saw the report myself, and the name given is 'unknown.' Same for the address. Nobody seemed sure whether that meant the rookies didn't get her name and address, or if the girl were suffering from amnesia and couldn't remember who she was or where she lived."

"Amnesia!" Brad's pulse raced at the idea. He hadn't even considered it before, but it would explain an awful lot. What if she'd gone for a walk in the park and been mugged...hit on the head...? Brad tried not to let his imagination run wild, but he couldn't help himself.

"Where did they take the girl?" he asked.

"To Bellevue. That much we do know for a fact."

"Then what are we waiting for?" Brad was already on his feet headed for the door.

"Hold on, Brad," Mike warned. He had caught the renewed excitement in Brad's manner and knew how dangerous it was. "Remember, I told you this one is a long shot."

"Then let's just say I'm a betting man."

"O.K., but you've got to have something to bet on. For all we now know the girl could have been brought in and released the next day. I could locate the cops for you first—have a talk with them, see what they remember. Maybe they can give us a description, although it's been a while. A lot of young girls have been picked up since then."

"Let's try the hospital first," Brad said decisively. "Then if she's been released we can always go to the cops."

"O.K., pal, we'll do it your way," Mike sighed, "but don't say later I didn't warn you."

It seemed to Brad as if the taxi would never get them across town to Bellevue Hospital. The traffic in midtown was snarled and congested like an angry crowd. If a bus wasn't blocking an intersection, then a delivery van or a block-long limousine was. And the traffic was only the first obstacle they faced. Brad knew from firsthand experience how difficult it was to penetrate the bureaucratic red tape in a hospital. But nothing had prepared him for the impenetrable sea of paper at Bellevue.

When they finally arrived at the hospital they went directly to the administration office, where a line of people was already waiting, clutching fists full of papers they couldn't understand. At best it would have been difficult to locate the girl they wanted, and the scantiness of their information made it almost impossible. Name, address, date of admission, illness—they knew none of the pertinent information.

"We're clutching at straws; you understand that, don't you?" Mike repeated his warning again as they waited for the records clerk to return.

"Maybe," Brad admitted. "But there is a possibility the girl is still here. Then her record would be in the active file. And if it's Leslie, then you have to presume that she was picked up the same day she disappeared and that she was suffering from memory loss. Even in a colossus like this place, that narrows down the number of patients we're talking about—probably to one."

"You should have been a private eye yourself." Mike shook his head. "You're beginning to think like one."

"It's not that," Brad admitted. "I've just had a lot of experience with hospitals, and they're all the same. Some are just bigger than others."

The records clerk came back as they were talking, a satisfied look on her face. "I can't even believe it myself," she said, slapping the file against her empty hand. "I thought it would be like looking for a needle in a haystack, but this might just be the patient you're looking for—an amnesiac, suffering from total memory loss. She knows she's not from New York, but that's about all she's sure of. Sorry I can't help you more than that. All I can do is give you her patient number and the name of her doctor. She's in the psychiatric ward, of course. You'll have to get the doctor's permission to visit her there."

It was several hours later before Brad finally succeeded in locating Dr. James Itoh and secured a pass to get into the psychiatric ward. Mike had gone back to the office by then to track down a different lead. Now, standing outside the locked and padded door of the mental ward while a husky nurse flicked through a big steel ring of keys, Brad felt his stomach turning over. Another trip on the emotional roller coaster, he thought grimly. And yet he kept going back to Dr. Itoh's description: "The girl doesn't seem unhappy. She hums to herself and often, when she thinks no one is watching, she drums her fingers along the tabletop, almost as if it were a piano. I've wondered many times if she played, but if I ask her directly, she becomes confused... disoriented."

The nurse glanced at Brad's pass as she opened the door. "She's a good patient, that one. No trouble to anyone," the nurse clucked approvingly. "Wish they were all that easy. Go straight down this corridor," she directed, pointing a thick, stubby finger. "Room 1837, fourth door on your right. When you want out, hit the buzzer right there. I'll come back and open up for you. Hey, good luck," she called after him.

"Thanks," Brad murmured as the door shut behind him.

For a moment he stood still, breathing deeply to steady himself. It wasn't just the possibility that the girl might be Leslie, it was the entire experience of being in a hospital again—in a psychiatric ward—that affected him so profoundly. It was such familiar ground. There had been a time when Brad had spent the better part of every day in the psychiatric ward of a major city hospital. A different lifetime really, and yet it came back to him in vivid detail as he started down the corridor.

The door to room 1837 was open and the occupant was seated at a table, a transparent plastic bag of different colored threads open beside her, weaving a potholder. Although her back was toward the door, Brad recognized the graceful angle of her head, the slender figure, the thick dark hair. His heart seemed to stop, and he murmured "Leslie," as if the word itself were a miracle.

Although the barest whisper had escaped from his lips, the girl turned around and looked up at him where he stood rooted in the doorway. It was Leslie, paler and thinner but unchanged except for the vacant expression in her eyes.

"Leslie," he repeated, afraid to frighten her and yet unable to contain his own joy. "It's Brad."

"Brad." She said the name thoughtfully as if it had touched some silent, hidden chord. But it was clear from her face that she didn't recognize him, didn't remember.

Brad knew that he shouldn't rush her. Years of intensive schooling had trained him to proceed slowly, to avoid causing renewed shock in the patient. But Leslie was not a case study. He could never look at her in clinical, impersonal terms. Impulsively, he rushed over to her and took both of her hands, pressing them to his lips. "You're Leslie Brooks and I'm Brad Elliot," he said fervently. "I've been looking everywhere for you. I love you. We were going to be married—and we still are if you can just remember who you are and who I am long enough to say 'I do.'"

The words rolled out, one after the other, like a song or a prayer—the very words that Leslie had so longed to hear and was sure she never would—so sure that she had blocked every memory out of her consciousness.

Now, suddenly, the blocks were falling. She searched Brad's face in amazement and uncertainty; knowing yet not knowing who he was, who she was. "Tell me again, please," she murmured.

Leslie didn't resist as he drew her up in front of him and circled her slender body with his arms pressing her head against his chest. She felt as if she were living out a dream and, at the same time, as if she had come home at last after a long, troubled journey. Why wasn't she afraid of him as she was of everyone else? Why did she let him hold her and feel so safe in his arms?

Listening to him repeat the words over and over—who she was and who he was and how much he loved her, each time adding something more about her family, her concerts, Genoa City—Leslie began to remember. At first she could only grasp fragments of ideas, pictures... But gradually she began to offer disconnected details for him to place.

Brad knew it would be a long process of recovery, but already she had made more progress than she had in all the weeks of hospitalization. With time and patience and endless love, Leslie would be his again—and this time he wouldn't let anyone or anything separate them.

Miracle cures rarely happen. Yet Leslie's memory returned so fast, now that she no longer wanted to forget, that in no time at all she was released from the hospital. It was a special day for both of them, and Brad planned it with care, allowing her plenty of time to rest between a shopping spree and dinner. They had a champagne supper in the elegant, panelled dining room of his hotel, lingering over dessert, only their fingertips touching across the damask tablecloth, after the other diners had gone.

Although he had reserved a separate room for her, afraid to rush her into anything yet, Leslie insisted on going upstairs with him. Until then they had only exchanged the chastest kiss. But locked in the privacy of his room, she yearned for more, and more, and more... Reluctant at first, then unable to resist her, Brad answered the deepest desire of her heart.

The engulfing fire, the glorious surrender to love filled the void that had been Leslie's life, making her whole again, restoring the trust, the joy, the dreams that had been shut out of her life for so long. It was as if they had never been separated, as if they had never been lost to one another.

Late in the night, too exhausted to do more, Brad and Leslie lay wrapped in each other's arms. There was so much still unsaid between them that sleep eluded them. Pride, misunderstanding, misguided love had broken them apart before.

Neither wanted to make the same mistake again.

"Will you marry me, Leslie?" Brad whispered against the shell of her ear.

"It's all I ever wanted."

"That makes two of us," he laughed. "They say love is blind, and we certainly were."

"I was afraid to ask you if you were tired of me or had found a new girl—if that was why you didn't want to get married. I didn't want you to feel you had to lie to spare my feelings," she confessed.

"I didn't want you to give up anything for my sake. I didn't want the responsibility," he admitted with equal candor.

"Everyone gives up something in a marriage," Leslie answered with a wisdom born of love, "and gains so much more. If only I'd been honest with you," she reflected, tracing patterns on his chest, "we'd be Mr. and Mrs. Bradley Elliot now."

"How could I expect you to be honest with me when I've hidden the truth from you since the first moment we met?"

"You don't have to tell me anything, Brad," she whispered reassuringly.

"I want to," he insisted. "I know now that I should have confessed to you a long time ago. It's a long story, and not a very pretty one, Leslie," he began. "And I won't blame you if you change your mind about me when I'm through."

"I'll never stop loving you, Brad," she vowed. Still, her body tensed against his, knowing that at last she was going to learn the mysteries that had always clung to Brad, separating them like an invisible curtain, closing her out of a part of his life.

Hugging her tighter against him, Brad closed his eyes and let the floodgates of his memory open wide.

"Before I came to Genoa City, before I met you, I had another separate life that you know nothing about, Leslie. I grew up in Wabash, Indiana, where my father was a general practitioner. I was proud to be the son of Dr. Elliot, the man whom everyone in town turned to with a problem, even if it wasn't a physical one. Doc Elliot's horse sense was at least as strong as his medical expertise, and ever since I can remember I wanted to grow up to be a doctor like my father. But adolescence created misunderstandings, driving a wedge between us. Even though I did go to medical school, the gap between us widened until we were no closer than strangers. I wouldn't allow any intimacy after that, and when I became a doctor myself I guarded my emotions, insulating myself from the pain I dealt with every day. I thought that if I allowed myself to feel the anguish of my patients, or guilt each time I failed to cure them, I would burn out. Maybe I built such an impregnable wall around my emotions that not even a woman who moved me deeply could penetrate it. And there was such a woman, Leslie. Her name was Barbara Anderson."

Brad paused, unsure how Leslie would take his revelations, yet determined to be honest with her at all costs. But she touched his cheek, a silent though unmistakable gesture for him to continue. Leslie wasn't surprised that there had been another woman in Brad's life before her. She wasn't even surprised that he was a doctor. Once he admitted his past profession, she wondered why she hadn't realized it herself. There had been so many indications, especially the understanding way he treated Chris, first after her rape, and then after her miscarriage.

Encouraged by Leslie's tacit response, Brad went on. "Barbara waited for years for me to answer her love. And in the end, instead of returning it, I destroyed her." He took a deep breath, gathering the strength to confess what he had done.

"Barbara was in nursing school when I was just beginning to establish myself as an up-and-coming neurosurgeon in Chicago. At that time, the last thing in the world I wanted to be saddled with was a wife and baby. You can imagine what happened. Barbara got pregnant. I insisted that she get an abortion. It's so easy to do now, I never thought another thing about it. I just assumed she'd done what I told her. When she dropped out of my life shortly afterward, I was relieved. She was looking for marriage, and I wasn't ready to settle down yet. I had completed a double specialization in neurosurgery and psychiatry, and was concentrating all my energies on building my practice.

Three years later Barbara came back into my life. She had finished her nursing training and was assigned to the operating room of the Chicago hospital where I was a rising young star. We took up where we left off. In no time Barbara was pressing for marriage again, and I was again holding her off.

"Looking back now, I think we would have gone on like that forever if it hadn't been for an accident." Brad's grip tightened around Leslie, drawing her closer to him as if he were afraid that he would lose her when she heard the rest of his story.

"I remember it as vividly now as if it were happening again. I was making my morning rounds when I heard myself being paged over the PA system: 'Emergency, Dr. Elliot. Please report to the O.R.' Instead of waiting for the elevator, I ran up the fire stairs and reached the operating room tense and winded. Barbara burst out of the scrub room, already dressed in her green gown and cap, and fell into my arms sobbing hysterically: 'There's been an accident—a terrible accident in the nursery school. If anything happens to him...'

"I shook her to force her to get a hold of herself, thinking that she should know better than to let herself fall to pieces when she might be needed in the operating room at any moment. Then I told her to pull herself together and tell me exactly what happened. 'My baby,' she cried, 'our baby, our son!'

"I stared at her, thinking she was having a nervous breakdown, then I realized what had happened. Instead of having an abortion, Barbara had gone away to have the baby. He would have been three then." Brad shut his eyes at the memory. "As we faced each other in anger, bitterness, and fear, the child was wheeled in. He was three years old, and he had suffered severe neurological damage in a freak accident at his nursery school. I felt as if fate had delivered him into my hands for a second time. The first time I wanted to end his life before it had even begun, and now I was being called upon to save him. To save the son I had never wanted. He was unconscious; still, I could see myself in him. The shape of his face, the color of his hair were the same as mine.

"But I touched him the first time not as a father, but as a surgeon. His spinal chord was severed. I knew that if he survived the operation, he would be crippled for life."

Brad stopped, but the tender pressure of Leslie's hand on his cheek gave him the courage to go on. "It was the most difficult operation I had ever performed. Nothing in all my training had prepared me to cut into the flesh of my own child. Once I made the initial incision, I worked like a machine to repair the damaged nerves, knowing even as I did that it was a useless task. Barbara stood by my side, handing me the instruments I needed. Her terror had turned to shock and she performed like a highly trained zombie. But as I started to close the incision, the boy's blood pressure dropped. His pulse stopped. The anesthesiologist warned me to start arrest procedures immediately to save the boy. I didn't.

"I stood, staring down at the tiny motionless figure lying under the powerful lights as quiet as death. Then I stripped off my bloody gloves, dropped them on the operating room floor, and turned away before anyone realized what I was doing. I just walked out—away from the hospital, away from Barbara, away from my career, my training, my practice, away from the son who had died beneath my hands."

Leslie's body had grown rigid beside him; still, Brad forced himself to go on. "All I heard as I walked away were Barbara's shattering screams: 'Murderer! You killed him! You killed my baby!'

I've been hearing those screams ever since."

Brad paused as if he couldn't bear to finish, but there were so many questions still unanswered that Leslie couldn't let him stop now.

"Did you go back, Brad?" she whispered in a hushed, barely audible boice. "Was your baby dead?"

"I didn't go back and the boy was dead," he answered flatly, exhaling a long plume of breath as if he'd been holding it back since he began his confession. "When I felt my son's life slipping away beneath my hands, I vowed never to pick up a scalpel again—never to accept the responsibility for another life. I gave up the thing that meant the most to me—my profession; and my one goal—to become the best neurosurgeon I could.

"I got in my car and began to drive with no objective except to put the life I had led up to that moment as far behind me as I could. Ironically, fate intervened. After driving for several hours, I stopped for coffee. When I was getting back into my car, I was mugged. The man must have followed me out of the restaurant, because just as I was unlocking the car door, he jumped me. I remember slumping down beside the car. When I regained consciousness, I had nothing. My wallet, ring, tie clip, and my car were all gone. The man didn't get far—only fifteen miles outside of Akron, but I didn't know that at the time.

"I hitched a ride with a truck driver bound for Genoa City. It was the end of his run, so I had no choice except to get out there. I was hungry and thirsty. Even though I didn't have a dime in my pocket, I went into what looked like a decent restaurant and ordered a steak. Luckily, your father was having lunch there at the same time. When I couldn't pay for my meal, he intervened with the manager, picked up the check, and offered me a job on his paper.

"Needless to say, I accepted gratefully. I'd been working on the newspaper for about two weeks handling the wire service reports when a story came in over the AP: Dr. Bradley Elliot, a Chicago neurosurgeon and psychiatrist, had been killed when his Corvette dovetailed on a slippery curve, crashed into a guard rail and caught fire. Identification was made from the license plate, ring, and tie clip—that was all that could be salvaged from the fire.

"There are not many men who read their own obituaries—or have a chance to begin their life a second time. But I did. The mugger, whoever he was, was buried in my place and I was free to start again. No one even knew Dr. Bradley Elliot still existed. And then I met you. For a long time I managed to convince myself that you never had to know about the other person I'd been. Now I know that there can't be any secrets between us, Leslie."

For a long time they lay side by side. Even though their bodies were touching, a heavy silence seemed to lie between them like an invisible barrier.

"Barbara should have told you about your son," Leslie murmured at last, deeply affected by Brad's story.

"I can't blame her. She knew I didn't want the baby. Back then I would have thought she was trying to trap me into marriage," he admitted.

"She loved you."

163

"Yes, I think she did, although at the time I didn't want to hear about love. I thought of it as just another word to tie me down."

For another long moment the only sound was Leslie's heavy breathing. Then, summoning up all her courage, she asked: "Did you love her, Brad? Did you love Barbara?"

He took Leslie's hand and held it against his heart, afraid that he was losing her again, yet wanting to be completely honest with her now that he had begun. "I guess I took Barbara for granted, sure that she would never turn away from me; yet I always avoided committing myself to her in any way. She said that I was afraid to love, and maybe she was right. I was afraid to allow myself to love—to commit myself to another person—until I met you. And then I loved you so much, I couldn't stand in your way. Don't you see, Leslie, I knew what it was like to give up the one thing I wanted most in the world, the one goal I had always striven for. That's why I called off our marriage. I didn't want to force you to give up your dream, as I had."

"And now?"

"Now that you know the dark, unforgivable secret I've been hiding from you, I can't blame you if you change your mind about me...about us. You fell in love with half a man."

"No, Brad." Leslie clung to his hand, knowing that whatever he had done, whoever he was, she would never stop loving him and feeling the depth of his suffering, his sorrow. "You've paid so much already. Are you going to keep on paying for the rest of your life?"

"I thought I would—until I met you and you

taught me how to love," he smiled, a trace of sadness still lingering around the corners of his mouth.

"And now you can teach me how to get better and be strong like you are, and learn to handle disappointment and even loss. You're better qualified than any doctor who's been treating me," Leslie offered.

"You'll never lose me again, Leslie," Brad vowed, taking her in his arms and kissing her eyes, which brimmed with tears for the woman and child Brad had lost. "But it's true. You have to become strong so that you're not dependent on anyone except yourself. Only then can you really be free to give your love to anyone—completely and forever. I don't want anything less than that from you, darling."

Chapter Eleven

Dreams Lost and Found

"Hello, Kay. It's good to see you being so industrious these days." Phillip Chancellor stood in the doorway of the solarium and smiled at his wife for the first time in years. Dressed in a bulky Irish sweater and plaid tam-o'-shanter, she was working industriously to plant spring bulbs before the ground froze entirely, a task she had been working at all week long. In fact, looking back, he calculated that she had begun just after the debacle at the club. "You even appear to be off the gin for the fifth straight day. Jill must be having a sobering effect on you at last."

"Sobering or otherwise, Jill Foster has had an effect on me—quite definitely," Kay responded icily.

"Where is Jill, by the way? I don't think I've seen her all week. Is she sick or something?" Phillip hated to ask his wife. But he hadn't seen Jill since the night they'd had such beautiful love together, and the tension was becoming unbearable. Had he hurt her in his ardor? Was she so filled with remorse and regrets that she couldn't bear to see him again? For five days Phillip had been tormenting himself with questions, until he'd become so anxious about her that he had to ask Kay.

"For your information, Phillip, Jill Foster is no longer in my employ. I fired her without notice or severance pay, and as long as I live in this house she will never set foot in it again. Is that perfectly clear?"

Only Phillip's eyes registered the shock he felt. He stood motionless in the doorway, staring at his wife as if she were a stranger—or worse. "Then you're not really better, are you Kay? No woman in her right mind would fire a jewel like Jill."

"Is that what she is, Phillip, a precious jewel?" Kay spat the words back at him scornfully. "Then you're the fool, not I. At best, Jill Foster is a rhinestone. A fake, and a tacky fake at that. I thought that at least you had good taste."

Phillip's fists clenched tightly at his sides, and his voice dropped a dangerous octave. "What are you talking about, Kay?" he demanded, his body as rigid as a board.

"Are you going to play the guiltless, misunderstood husband? I don't think the part suits you, dearest, or maybe I just know you too well for too many years to be taken in."

"You don't know me at all, Kay."

"Maybe you're right." She began digging a hole for a tulip bulb, throwing up the soil as if it were a lethal enemy she was determined to root out. "I certainly never expected you to be so coarse, so...so goddamned *indecent*," she finished, unable to hide the fury that was seething in her heart.

"I think you'd better tell me exactly what you're getting at," Phillip demanded.

"Oh, don't play the holy innocent with me," she charged fiercely. "I'm talking about the disgusting affair you're having with that...that rhinestone."

"I'm not having an affair with anyone, Kay. I thought that was your specialty."

"There's no point in denying it. I saw you, Phillip. I watched you with that Foster person. You dropped me at the door after the country club dance as if I had some contagious disease and snuck out to the cabana with her." Kay watched the color drain from her husband's face with a perverse pleasure. She wanted to hurt him as acutely as he had hurt her, to make him suffer for his disloyalty.

"Why did you do that, Kay?" His face was white with an ice-cold fury that paled even his lips, and his voice was low and menacing in its extreme control.

"Why did I do it?" she stormed. "You should be the one answering that question."

"Jill and I are not having an affair. That was the first time—the only time. I wanted to, but she refused me on the grounds that it was disloyal to you. She didn't want to sneak around behind your back, to have to pretend to you. That's the kind of girl Jill Foster is—a kind of woman you could never understand."

"Saint Jill," Kay jeered. "I don't think there is one, so you can put her up for canonization. Really, Phillip, I am impressed by your chivalry.

You probably would have made a divine knight in shining armor if we were living in the Middle Ages, but you make a damned pathetic liar."

"It's the truth, Kay," he insisted tensely through clenched teeth.

"My royal arse it is," she swore. "Shall I tell you how she looked? But of course you remember, don't you?

"Stop it, Kay!" he commanded, and the ice-cold anger in his tone was so glacial that for a moment she seemed to shrink back from it. "I won't listen to another word from you. Only a sick, sick woman would do what you apparently did. I want a divorce—as soon as possible. I should have insisted on it years ago."

"I'll never grant you one," she vowed.

"Don't force me to divorce you, Kay. We can at least preserve some dignity in public, even if none remains between us."

"No! I won't let you cast me aside so that you can go running to that cheap little manicurist. She's nothing. She'll always be nothing."

"I intend to marry Jill, if she'll have me, as soon as our divorce becomes final."

Phillip's declaration fell between them like a time bomb, the seconds on it ticking away with mounting danger.

"Over my dead body," Kay swore viciously. "I will fight you every step of the way—and don't think you can plead an alcoholic wife. I haven't had a drink since that enlightening evening."

It was true. Kay no longer had any need for booze. She had something to live for now other than a liquor bottle. She was determined to drive

Jill out of her husband's life. She was Mrs. Phillip Chancellor, and she intended to remain Mrs. Phillip Chancellor for as long as she lived. The torrid affairs she had carried on with the stableboys were nothing compared to her husband's infidelity. They were no different from the tarts she knew Phillip occasionally paid for since he had barred her from his bed. But Jill Foster was very different. Kay felt as if a daughter had betrayed her, and now Phillip was prepared to marry Jill. She would never allow it, any more than she would forget or forgive the scene she had witnessed in the cabana.

"I won't give her up, Kay," Phillip was saying. "Jill is everything you're not. She's warm and loving and caring. Even at your best," he added, cruelly turning the knife, "you were none of those things."

Kay forced a hard, derisive laugh, even though her husband's words had found their mark with stinging accuracy. "She's young and she has a nice body. They're her only assets. Beyond that she's a scheming, conniving little witch, and you're either too blind or too stupid to see it. What do you think Jill Foster wants from you? Your glorious, virile young body? You're old enough to be her father. She wants what you have—luxury, wealth, this house, the servants. She wants to be a *grande dame*... mistress of the manor. Haven't you noticed the way she strutted around here as if she already owned it? You just go along with the furnishings."

"I won't hear another word of your slander, Kay." Phillip's voice was as hard and unyielding as his stance as he turned his back on her. "I want a divorce and that's final. If you haven't contacted a lawyer by next week, then I'll leave orders for my attorney to give you a list of names. I don't want to drag your pathetic, destructive behavior through a public courtroom. But if you force me to, I will. You haven't exactly been discreet yourself, you know," he added coldly.

"I won't let you get away with this, Phillip. You've been my husband for thirty years..."

"Thirty wretched years," he interrupted.

"They weren't all bad. You have to admit *that* at least," she said, her tough, vengeful attitude weakening for a moment. "Not in the beginning, anyway."

"It's been a loveless marriage for a long time, Kay. There's no point in pretending between ourselves."

"I admit I haven't always been a perfect wife...or a perfect mother to Brock for that matter. Still, it's a little late in the game to switch hitters, don't you think?"

"I try to think of you as little as possible, Kay," he replied with savage honesty. "I've found it's less painful that way."

Phillip Chancellor was not naturally a cruel man. For a long, trying decade he had suffered through his wife's alcoholism, her embarrassing drunken displays, and her blatant affairs with extraordinary patience, because he remembered the woman he had married. Through the years, though, as she continued to drink, any lingering affection he might have felt dried up like a riverbed in a drought, so that now they shared only a house and possessions—nothing more. Even their son was gone far from their reach.

Phillip's bitter words brought tears to Kay's eyes, but she blinked them away quickly, refusing to allow her husband to see that he could still touch her heart, that she had felt his words as sharply as a knife.

"Remember to contact a lawyer tomorrow, Kay, unless you want me to do it for you," he warned, turning his back on her without another glance.

"Where are you going, Phillip?" she screamed after his retreating figure.

"To find Jill and ask her to marry me," he said, without bothering to look back.

"You'll never get away with this," Kay swore after him. "I'll destroy you both before I'll see you married to Jill Foster."

Gwen blinked and squinted against the sun that streamed in her hospital room window. Shading her eyes, she looked around her as she remembered what had happened and where she was. Sometime while she was still unconscious, she had been moved from the emergency room and placed in a semi-private room, bigger and brighter than her own apartment. The bed beside hers was empty, and judging by the view through the bank of windows—an undisturbed vista of brilliant blue sky and startlingly white clouds— she was on a high floor. Once her eyes became adjusted to the sunlight, she saw a huge arrangement of chrysanthemums—russet, yellow, gold, and white—on the bureau, and a figure seated in the lounge chair beside it, a magazine opened but unread on his lap.

The little hint of color that had returned to

Gwen's cheeks faded as she stared at him, uncertain and unwilling to relive the terrible scene they had enacted on the street the night before.

"Greg," she gasped, and turned quickly away, embarrassed by what she was and why she was there.

Seeing that she was awake, Greg went over to the bed and smiled down at her, kissing her tenderly on the forehead. "Don't try to talk now, darling. Snapper said you should conserve what little strength you have, and there'll be lots of time later to tell me everything that happened."

"Darling!" Gwen thought in confusion. Greg called me "darling." But aloud she said: "Snapper—the doctor. He promised not to tell you."

"I know, but I'd never forgive myself if anything happened to you on my account."

"But last night..."

"Last night I didn't know what you were doing there. You should have told me."

"I couldn't," she faltered. "*He* was watching us. He told me he would be. You have to stay away from me or he'll hurt you, too. Promise me you will." She grasped his hand and clung to it, pleading.

"Shhh," Greg soothed. "I'm supposed to be keeping you quiet. Besides, I have a better way to deal with this Duke whatever-his-name-is."

"Duke Stevens." Gwen whispered the name as if, even by speaking it, she was courting danger for them both.

"Duke Stevens. There's a law against aggravated assault and battery, you know. A law that will take bullies like Duke Stevens off the streets and put them in jail where they belong. Then you won't have to be frightened of him anymore. You could begin again, Gwen—make a fresh start as if none of this had ever happened, and you were arriving in Genoa City for the first time. Instead of Duke Stevens, you meet me," Greg went on, letting his dreams carry him away.

"Do you mean it, Greg?" she asked, afraid to hope again, and yet enchanted by the fairy tale he was weaving for them.

"Every word of it," he laughed, believing in what he had said, and, also believing in them—the two of them—again. "But it all depends on you, Gwen."

She searched his face with wide, bewildered eyes, wondering what she could do to make their dreams come true. When she was released from the hospital she knew that Duke Stevens would be waiting for her at the front gate, lounging nonchalantly against the wall, his silver Cadillac parked at the curb, ready to claim what he owned. "Duke will never let us get away with it," Gwen said, shaking her head bleakly. "Never. He'll kill us first. That's just the kind of rat he is."

"Only if you let him, Gwen. It's up to you. All I can do is help."

In the corridor outside, nurses rushed from room to room, answering buzzers, dispensing medication. New visitors arrived; doctors stopped by on their rounds. But Gwen's room was silent. Although he didn't want to pressure her, knowing that there was always an element of danger involved, Greg prayed that Gwen would do what he wanted. Otherwise, she was right. That leech would be waiting for her, and the whole vicious cycle would begin again—until one day Gwen would be wheeled into the hospital again. Only the next time it would be too late to save her.

Gwen looked up at him, conflicting emotions of trust and fear visible in her drawn, white face. "What do you want me to do, Greg?" she asked in a small, scared voice.

"I want you to press criminal charges against Duke Stevens on the grounds of aggravated assault and battery. That means the police will be able to pick him up and throw him in the can—at least until he can post bail."

The fear in Gwen's voice turned to terror. "Then he'll really come after us," she whispered.

"No," Greg promised, hoping that he could keep his word, certain that it was the only chance to save Gwen—the only chance either of them had. "You're going to stay someplace where Duke can't reach you until all this is over and he's locked up in a prison cell. But it won't be easy for you, Gwen. You'll have to go to court and testify in front of a judge and jury about exactly what he did to you. And all the time, he'll be sitting right there too, staring at you, trying to frighten you into silence."

Gwen listened, trying even now to keep herself from trembling. "Where will you be, Greg?" she asked finally.

"Right there beside you every moment, if that's what you want," he swore.

Although she tried to smile, she found herself shaking her head instead. "I don't think I can," she admitted hopelessly, "even if you're there. I'd be so scared for you."

"Don't think of me or you," Greg told her.

"Think of all the other girls you'd be helping. Fifteen-year-old kids, just like you were once, lonely and frightened. Just the kind of kid Duke Stevens watches for, like a fox stalking a chicken. You know better than I the life you'd be saving them from, Gwen."

The hospital chaplain knocked on the door, then poked his head in just as Gwen was about to reply. Her immediate reaction was to send him away. "I can't talk to a man of God—not after what I've done," she whispered to Greg. "Send him away. *Please.*"

"Maybe he's just the person you should talk to, Gwen," Greg suggested instead. "He may be able to help you in ways I can't."

"I'm too ashamed," she murmured. "I can't." But Greg had already gotten up and was slipping out of the room.

At the door he turned back and blew her a kiss, grinning at the guilty, trapped expression on her face. But if Gwen had expected the chaplain to preach a sermon to her, she was due for a surprise. He was kind, understanding, and above all sympathetic, and after a few minutes with him Gwen began to relax. For the first time she had found someone to whom she could confess everything—holding nothing back as she had from Greg—and still be assured of forgiveness.

Chapter Twelve

New Horizons

"Ten to twenty years with no time off for good behavior—I'll drink to that," Greg grinned, raising a glass of wine to toast Gwen. "Now you don't have to be afraid anymore. Duke Stevens is going to be locked up in a place where he can't touch you—or any of the other girls in his stable."

An hour before, the jury in the case of Gwendolyn Sherman v. Duke Stevens had come back with a verdict of guilty as charged. It marked the end of an agonizing and terrifying ordeal for Gwen. To sit in the courtroom day after day with Duke's venomous eyes fixed on her, burning with vengeance...to have to answer the most intimate, sordid questions in public under intense, often cruel cross-examination had been a harrowing experience. Now that it was over, her relief was so great that she felt as if she'd been released from a life sentence herself. She wanted to cry and laugh at the same time.

"I never could have gotten through it without you, Greg," she said, clicking her glass against his so that the crystal rang like chimes. "You can't imagine what a terrible coward I am inside. Every morning when I woke up I had to force myself to get out of bed, put on my clothes, and make my feet carry me back to the courthouse. Just seeing Duke there watching me...being so near him..." Gwen shuddered at the memory.

"You don't have to think about him anymore," Greg insisted, leaning closer to her. "That part of your life is over—wiped out as if it never existed," he added vehemently. "You were tremendous on the witness stand. Just remember that and forget all the rest. Today is a new beginning —for both of us."

Leaning back against the leather banquette, Gwen smiled lovingly at him. "You've been so good to me, Greg. I never would have had the courage to press charges against Duke if it hadn't been for you—you and Chaplain Cronin."

Greg frowned. Gwen never failed to surprise him. "Who's Chaplain Cronin?"

"You remember, he was the chaplain in the hospital. Actually, you were the one who made me talk to him in the first place. And he's taught me so much I didn't know about myself...and about God." Gwen blushed, as embarrassed by her spiritual awakening as she had been by her sexual abasement.

"Hold it," Greg teased. "You make this Chaplain Cronin sound so great, I think I should be getting jealous."

"He's a very special friend," Gwen answered with total seriousness. "I wanted to tell you about him before, and introduce you. But I was afraid you'd laugh at me or something. He was with me all the way through the trial, but he told me not to force myself to do anything. When it felt comfortable for me, he would meet you."

"You mean Chaplain Cronin was that guy who sat in the front row every day in the plain gray suit? You kept turning back to look at him and smile at him all the time?"

Gwen was nodding to each of his questions.

"What a jerk I was," Greg grimaced. "I thought he was one of your old customers—that's why I was afraid to ask you."

Gwen smiled. "He'll enjoy hearing that. Because he says that every one of us is part saint, part sinner. That's why we should never judge each other, no matter what we do. 'There but for the grace of God...' I feel as if I've been given a new life, a new beginning. It's the most precious gift, and I want to show how grateful I am for it each day."

"You're not kidding, are you?" Greg exclaimed in amazement.

"I've never been more serious about anything. Chaplain Cronin has given a meaning to my life."

"You mean you've found God?"

"I've found someone whom I know has always loved me and cared for me, no matter what I've done. Chaplain Cronin calls Him 'God'." Gwen's voice was soft yet intense.

It was early yet for most diners, and the stillness of the restaurant closed around them like a cocoon. Greg gazed at her, still unable to overcome his surprise. Her eyes shone brightly with a new-found peace and contentment.

"You're different, Gwen," he said with undisguised wonderment. Wrapped up in the intense work of the trial, he hadn't noticed the change in her. "You'll never go back to your old life again, will you?"

"No. I couldn't, not now. Even though I know that God would forgive me, I couldn't disappoint Him like that."

Greg felt as if his deepest wish had come true. He still loved Gwen, but he'd been afraid that one day she might slip back into her old ways. Now he believed that she had changed. She would never go back to the street again. She would be his—only his, 'until death do us part.' Reaching for her hand, he pressed it to his lips, kissing each finger with utmost tenderness.

"Today truly will be a new beginning for us, Gwen," he smiled, his eyes filled with happiness. "Now we can be married—just as we had planned."

"Greg," Gwen began slowly, closing her fingers over his. "You know that I love you. I'll always love you. I owe so much to you I can never begin to repay you."

"When you marry me," he teased, "I'll make sure to collect on that debt every hour on the hour."

"No, Greg," she stopped him, "hear me out— please. I've thought about this so much—all through the trial. There's only one way I can repay my debts to everyone who has believed in me, helped me, and saved me from the sordid life I was leading. There's only one way to thank God for His forgiveness."

"I don't understand, Gwen, what you're trying

to say," Greg shook his head in puzzlement. "I think you're saying that you love me, but..."

"I do love you, Greg. I've told you that, and I mean it with all my heart. But I love Him as well. Since Chaplain Cronin brought me back to God, I feel like a child who has found her Father after years of being an orphan. He's been there all the time, but I didn't see Him. Now I want to make up for all the time I lost."

"I don't understand what any of that has to do with marrying me," Greg admitted. "If you're afraid I'd stand in the way of your new religion..." he began to object.

"Of course not," she assured him, giving his hand a last squeeze. "I think you'll be a wonderful husband to the girl you finally marry."

Uncomprehending, Greg stared at her. "What do you mean—the girl I finally marry?"

"What I've been trying to tell you, Greg, is that I've made up my mind to devote the rest of my life to God—to make up for all that I've done against Him. I've talked with Chaplain Cronin about it, and he's willing to arrange a way for me to join a convent of women who are united in their love and commitment to work for God. When you urged me to press charges against Duke, you told me to think about all the other homeless kids like myself I'd be saving. And I have—I've thought about them a lot. Now I want to spend the rest of my life trying to help them, to show them that they *do* have a choice. They don't have to be dependent on men like Duke."

Greg sat in amazement as Gwen explained her plan, marveling at the new strength she had discovered within herself, yet weeping inside for the girl he would never have again. "I love you, Gwen," he murmured brokenly. "Doesn't that mean anything to you?"

"It means more than I can ever tell you. It was your love that started me going straight in the first place. It was your love that brought me to Chaplain Cronin, and I will always cherish it. But I feel that it would be selfish to marry you. I'd only be thinking of my own happiness—and I want to think of others too. Of all those other lonely, frightened, desperate girls you made me remember. Please, Greg, try to understand. I would never willingly hurt you."

Greg swallowed the tears that threatened to choke him, but he couldn't destroy the happiness that shone in Gwen's face as she talked about her own new beginning. He loved her so much that it filled his heart with warmth—as well as a terrible sadness —to see the change in her. "I love you so much, Gwen, that your happiness means everything to me."

"Then be happy for me, Greg, because I feel sure that for the first time in my life, I'm doing the right thing."

Greg forced himself to smile for her sake. "I am, Gwen," he answered, looking longingly at the flame-haired beauty he had come to love so deeply.

"Come on down and take a break. You're working much too hard," Brad called up to Leslie, who was perched on the highest rung of an eight-foot stepladder, painting the molding around the ceiling.

"O.K., Brad, I can use one." She scrambled

down, surveying the job she had done with
satisfaction. So much had happened to her since
Brad had found her in New York that Leslie felt
caught up in a whirlwind of happiness.

Her homecoming had been filled with such
love that she was still basking in the warmth of it.
All the Brookses were waiting to greet her with
tears and embraces when Brad brought her back
to Genoa City: Chris and Snapper, Peggy, and
her parents. Everyone except Laurie. No one
mentioned her except to say that she had decided
to return to Paris for a visit, and Leslie didn't ask
for more details. One day she would confront her
sister, but she wasn't ready yet. First, she had
more healing to do.

"If you'd waited, I would have done that
painting for you on my day off," Brad said,
planting a kiss on the tip of her paint-speckled
nose.

"I like to do it," she smiled, trying not to touch
him for fear of getting him spotted too, but
finding it difficult to resist the temptation.
"Anyway, you told me I have to learn to be
independent. That's an important part of my
therapy, isn't it?"

"*I'm* the important part of your therapy," he
said, looking at her lustfully. Leslie wore worn
jeans with a baseball cap pulled over her hair to
catch the paint, but he thought she was the most
irresistible woman he'd ever seen.

"I agree," she murmured, reaching up for
another kiss.

"You'd better be careful," he teased. "If you
keep that up, I just may not go back to the office

at all. Then you won't have a chance to finish your painting."

"This place is really beginning to shape up, don't you think?" she asked eagerly. "Today, for the first time, I can see how it will look."

On Brad's advice, Stuart Brooks had bought Frenchy's Restaurant for his eldest daughter—to give her a new outlet for her talent, a way to become independent and at the same time learn to express herself and her feelings more fully. Since Pierre Rolland's death, the restaurant had stood vacant. Sally McQuire had moved to Chicago, and Pierre's sister Marie, after trying unsuccessfully to run the place alone, had shuttered the doors again. Now Leslie and her mother were transforming Frenchy's into a nightclub. When the renovations were complete, it would reopen as the Allegro Café, featuring Leslie Brooks as a cabaret-style singer.

The idea of a singing career had been Brad's brainstorm. In spite of the enormous progress she had made, he didn't feel that Leslie was ready to resume the grueling concert tour schedule. It was important for her to be home, surrounded by people who loved and supported her. And selfishly, Brad didn't want her to leave him again. Singing at her own cabaret would utilize her musical talents without burdening her with the pressures a concert pianist faced. It seemed like the perfect compromise—an interim step that would restore her confidence in her own performing talent after her shaky concert tour and, at the same time, allow her a breathing period to decide her own future.

"The Allegro Café—Leslie Brooks performing!"

Brad mimed as if he were reading a marquee. "When your father bought this place, I wasn't sure you were ready to take such a big step. I thought of it more as an insurance for you to have in the future."

"And now?"

"I think you're sensational—and in a few weeks everyone else in Genoa City will discover what I already know." His dark eyes roamed what had once been the main dining room of Frenchy's and came to rest on her glowing face, penetrating the deepest recesses of her heart with the intensity of his gaze.

"You mean it, don't you?" Leslie cried exuberantly, forgetting her paint-covered clothes and throwing her arms around his neck. She smelled of turpentine and paint thinner, on her a sweeter perfume than any scent bottled in the most expensive cut-crystal, and Brad knew that every day without Leslie as his wife—to wake up with, to go home to, to share each moment with—was another lost day in his life.

"Kiss me again if you love me," she murmured, her lips already yearning toward his. She was so shy, so reserved, so ethereal, yet she made love with a fiery intensity, a total lack of inhibition. Her passion was a constant surprise to him.

And he did, knowing that once he began to kiss her, he wouldn't be able to stop himself.

Her hands slid under his jacket, caressing his back.

"I brought a picnic for us," he said huskily. "Aren't you hungry?"

"Very hungry...for you."

"What if the workmen come back?"

She knew he was protesting only to heighten their anticipation. "They won't. They're not working until tomorrow."

"I have to cover the mayor's press conference in half an hour."

"Then why are you wasting time talking?" she laughed daringly.

"Marry me today, and we'll have all night," he urged impulsively, pulling her close.

"We can't cheat Mother out of another wedding—not after all I've put her through."

"Is a week enough time to plan a wedding?" Brad teased.

Leslie shook her head. "I wish it were."

"Two weeks? Four weeks?"

"Make it six weeks from today," she laughed happily. "Mother will have to work miracles. I can't wait that long, though," she admitted hungrily. "I want you so much."

"Show me how much," Brad urged, his voice low and sensual. "Take what you want—all that you want. I can never run out of love for you," he vowed. Her past anguish was forgotten; Leslie had her true love at last, now and forever.

When Brad went back to the office, his shirtfront was stained with paint—a dusky, gray-blue hue. Brad didn't care, because it was like a special mark on a calendar reminding him of a special day. In fact, he would have been happy to wear it for the next six weeks—until the day that he and Leslie had set for their wedding. And this time there would be no delays and no postponements.

YOU CAN NOW ORDER PREVIOUS
TITLES OF *SOAPS & SERIALS*™ BOOKS
BY MAIL

Just complete the order form and detach on the dotted line and send together with your check or money order payable to *SOAPS & SERIALS*:

SOAPS & SERIALS™
120 Brighton Road, Box 5201
Clifton, NJ 07015-5201

Please circle the books you wish to order:

THE YOUNG AND THE RESTLESS	BK # 1 2 3
DAYS OF OUR LIVES	1 2 3
GUIDING LIGHT	1 2 3
ANOTHER WORLD	1 2 3
AS THE WORLD TURNS	1 2 3
CAPITOL™	1 2 3
DALLAS™	1 2 3
KNOTS LANDING™	1 2 3

Each book is $2.50 ($3.25 in Canada).

Total number of books circled _____
   @ $2.50   ($3.25 Canada) $_____
Sales tax (CT residents only) $_____
Shipping and Handling $_____.95
Total payment enclosed (checks or
   money orders only) $_____

Name _____
Address _____ Apt. # _____
City _____
State _____ Zip _____
Telephone No. _____